# Left Out

## Alternative Policies for a Left Opposition Today

**Doug Bain**

**Peter Lawrence**

**Andy Pearmain**

**Michael Prior**

**Willie Thompson**

ISBN: 978-1-4457-8182-2

# Contents

# Introduction

The election on 6 May has thrown British politics into something of a frenzy with much talk of a new era of constitutional reform and a new kind of politics. In fact, in cold statistical terms there was little that was new or unusual in this election. There was a swing between the two main parties that was large but by no means unprecedented. Its main feature was that the arrow on the swinging wheel-of-fortune that has been British electoral politics stopped in the no-mans-land between a clear majority for either party. Again, unusual but not unprecedented and something that will happen regularly even in first-past-the-post systems. The number of seats held by other than Labour or Conservatives was, historically, rather large but this number was actually decreased by the election. There was no upsurge of new political groups; the LibDems dropped their representation; the nationalist parties trod water and various independents were wiped out.

The unusual feature of the election was really its context rather than its result; a widespread feeling that the election was about the very nature of British governance, a suggestion that we were seeing a crisis in the legitimacy of the system rather than the accustomed passing of power from one of the parties to the other. The election's outcome did not confirm this nor did it wholly deny it. It may be seen in the years to come as a warning from the electorate to try harder. The formation of the Tory/LibDem coalition suggests that one part of the political establishment is doing

3

just that. Its success is yet to be proven and British politics could still be in for the turbulent period that many believed would be the result of 6 May.

This may yet be so but one thing is already clear; that the British left was sidelined during the election campaign and had very little influence on whatever solution is found for what, quite clearly, is a painful dilemma for the British ruling elite. Inside and outside the Labour Party, left groups were left groping for any clear response to the sudden emergence of another centre-left group, resorting mostly to the an old 'hold-your-nose and vote Labour to keep the Tories out' unless, in the case of those outside Labour, their own faction was standing to receive votes which were, in the event, largely derisory.

This is a crude, perhaps a rather cruel summary of the complex, sometimes tortured debate which took place inside some left circles. But politics is a cruel business and the fact remains that the most constructive response which many on the left found was essentially negative; to vote for any candidate they found on the ballot who was not Labour and who was nominally on the left, simply to increase the popular vote against the two-party stranglehold on British politics.

The essays in this book have been written to provide some longer perspective on the crisis of the British left and offer come constructive solutions derived from this perspective. They have an historical bias because most of the problems of the left derive from long-term issues which remain unresolved, some not even confronted. But their purpose is not to write history, it is to provide some pointers to the future.

# The Left in Scotland

# Doug Bain

## *Breaking Up*

The United Kingdom is breaking up. This is not
something that might happen depending on future
political developments in Scotland, Wales and
Northern Ireland. It is happening now. Political
trajectories in England, Scotland, Wales and N
Ireland are rapidly diverging. Whether this process
ends in separate, independent nations remains to be
seen; but the direction of travel is now clear. A
Scottish Social Attitudes Survey in mid January
2010 showed that 69% of Scots favour increased
powers for Holyrood – a figure unlikely to have
decreased following the result of the general
election. In Scotland even the unionist parties now
agree that devolution is an ongoing process and
that Scotland should be taking more control over
its own affairs. While Wales started from a
different baseline, the parallels with what is
happening in Scotland are broadly similar.
Northern Ireland is slowly and painfully
overcoming its sectarian divisions and will
increasingly see its future as part of Ireland rather
than Britain.

The days of debating the future of a British left are
over – there will be no more 'British Roads to
Socialism'. In Scotland and Wales, the process of
coming to terms with this major change is now
fairly well advanced. A significant section of the
left supports independence – the Scottish National

Party, the Scottish Socialist Party, Tommy Sheridan's Solidarity Party and the Green Party. The Scottish Labour and Conservative parties are strongly opposed, the Scottish LibDems support a 'federalist' option - but one which is firmly in the unionist camp. The Scottish Trades Union Congress remains for the moment broadly agnostic. But the argument is in full flow.

The outcome of the 2010 general election is unlikely to slow down the process of separation. England clearly voted Tory; Scotland clearly voted Labour. The LibDem/Conservative coalition will inevitably be perceived as lacking legitimacy in Scotland. Scotland voted Labour, not out of any particular enthusiasm for Gordon Brown's government, but to register its opposition to the return of a Tory government pledged to cutting social services. But that tactic failed and increasingly people in Scotland will be questioning the point of voting in UK elections. To make matters worse, the coalition government is committed to resolving the 'West Lothian question' by restricting the voting rights of Scottish MPs at Westminster thus further undermining the legitimacy of the Union in Scottish eyes.

 Having said that, it could turn out that the Tories, with less to lose in Scotland, will adopt a less virulently hostile attitude to the SNP government than Labour. Within weeks of taking office, the new government has announced that it will deliver on the recommendations of the Calman Commission – something the Labour government has been blocking for two years. But when the full £1b package of cuts is imposed on Scotland – probably in 2011 – it is likely that the powers conceded by Calman will be seen as a totally inadequate defence of Scotland's interests and pressure will grow for full fiscal autonomy and independence. The United Kingdom is likely to become increasingly ungovernable.

The left in England has been slow to adjust to the breaking up of the Union. For most, the 'peripheral' nations rarely make it on to their radar screens. The left Labour *Compass* group is a good example of this myopia. In 2006, as part of a renewal of politics project, they published a document entitled *The Good Society*[1]. Scotland and Wales each get one mention in the 70 odd pages – Northern Ireland is ignored altogether. Even in the chapter entitled *A Positive Internationalism* there is no mention of the nations making up the Union. In the three TV leader debates in the run up to the general election, once again the focus was entirely on England with no acknowledgement on the part of the speakers that health, education, law and order, local government have been devolved to the Scottish parliament.

But even when the issue is addressed by the English left, the attitude to break-up is usually hostile. Eric Hobsbawm was recently interviewed in the *New Left Review*.[2] He is quite scathing about all the little nations which have become independent since 1945 – places like Andorra and Luxembourg *and all the rest (who) weren't even reckoned as part of the international system, except by stamp collectors.....It is also quite clear that, in terms of power, these states are not capable of*

---

[1] Compass: *The Good Society* Lawrence and Wishart. 2006
[2] Eric Hobsbawm *World Distempers*. New Left Review No 61. Jan/Feb 2010

*playing the part of traditional states – they do not possess the capacity to make war against other states. They've become fiscal paradises or useful sub-bases for transnational dealers. Iceland is a good example; Scotland is not far behind.* For Eric, Scottish and English nationalism both represent the rise of a dangerous cultural xenophobia.

But things are changing. Mark Perryman has recently produced *Breaking Up Britain – Four Nations after a Union* arguing that *devolution has begun to burst apart this conspiracy of a Greater Englishness masquerading as Britishness*.[3] He argues cogently that the process of break-up could well fuel a resurgence of a right-wing nationalism in England. David Runciman, writing in the London Review of Books[4], argues that when the going gets tough for the new coalition government, the Tories may be tempted to play the nationalist card in England to shore up support.

But perhaps we should be clear about what exactly is breaking up. The nations of the United Kingdom share a very long common history. Whether Scotland opts for independence or 'devolution max', there is no doubt that Scotland-England cooperation and partnership across a wide range of functions will continue. What is breaking up is the British *state* with Scotland, Wales and Northern Ireland increasingly taking control over their own affairs. It is common, as a kind of short-hand, to

---

[3] Mark Perryman. *Breaking Up Britain* Lawrence & Wishart. London 2009

[4] David Runciman: *Is this the End of the UK*. LRB 27th May 2010

describe the past 50 years as characterised by the 'rise of Scottish nationalism'. However this is entirely misleading. Scotland has been a nation for a thousand years. The national identity of the Scottish people is powerfully rooted and fully articulated. It has never waned despite the 'British' overlay. It has never suffered a crisis of confidence – it had no need to 'rise' and do anything. The movement of the last half century has not been about retrieving a lost national identity: it has been about the recovery of statehood. And that's where the 'loss' has been – a loss that has run like a thread through Scottish life for 300 years. As Tom Nairn puts it: *The recovery of a collective will by an already constituted nation is not at all the same as 'nation building' in the sense made familiar through the annals of ethnic nationalism and decolonisation.*[5] Scotland had been a nation-state for more than 800 years before the Act of Union. That is not something easily erased from the collective memory. When Winnie Ewing opened the first session of the Scottish Parliament in 1999 she famously announced that the parliament, dissolved in 1707, was hereby 're-convened'. The word resonated across Scotland. So what is involved here is not some kind of national liberation; it is about the break-up of the British state as a consequence of Scotland re-establishing its own parliament. It is about democratic renewal. It has nothing whatsoever to do with xenophobia. Scottish and English nationalisms are two very different kettles of fish.

---

[5] Tom Nairn: *After Britain.* Granta Books London 2001 (p. 13)

Left Out: Policies for a Left Opposition

It is manifestly clear that the establishment of devolved parliaments in Scotland and Wales has led to national and cultural renaissance. The nationalist parties of Scotland and Wales and Northern Ireland are broadly left of centre and provide some kind of political alternative to that of the unionist Parties. Despite the recession, there is available an alternative vision for the future. For the Scots and Welsh, breakup will be experienced as a political and cultural enhancement.

For England, the implications are less clear. While the Scots have struggled for 300 years to articulate and conserve their Scottish identity *vis-à-vis* a dominant neighbour, English identity, in contrast, has been powerfully fashioned by her imperial past. A significant element of current English nationalism is a feeling of loss. As Tom Nairn puts it, *England is now a country in its afterlife; unable either to revive its pre-eminence or resign itself to loss*[6]. Scottish secession, in particular, will tend to be viewed as an unfriendly and disloyal act. In a recent poll by NatCen, 33% of English people thought Scotland was being subsidised by England; but, paradoxically, only 19% thought Scotland should become independent. Significant sections of the English feel their national identity is being threatened – by European integration, immigration and now the possible secession of Scotland. The main thrust of Perryman's book is that the English left should welcome the breakup of a corrupt and over-centralised British state and should engage in defining a progressive version of English national identity.

---

[6] Tom Nairn. *Triumph of the Termites.* London Review of Books, April 8th 2010

10

## *Identifying the Scottish Left.*

Possibly the most encouraging outcome of the general election, as far as England is concerned, has been the failure of the right to capitalise on the recession. Contrary to expectations, the BNP suffered a significant set-back. The LibDem government itself clearly represents a setback for the Tory right wing as Cameron unites with the LibDems to shift his party to the centre. The problem for the left in England is that we now have all three main parties competing for the centre ground.

Prospects for the left in Scotland are significantly more positive though also more complicated. The unionist/independence dichotomy cuts across and increasing overshadows the traditional left/right divide. In what follows, I will try to make an assessment of the current state of health of the Scottish left and at the same time attempt to identify some of the key elements of the new politics.

## *Context*

One crucial consequence of devolved government in the UK has been to create a pluralist left. While it is valid to attempt to define generalised principles and values, in practice the left in Scotland will powerfully reflect Scotland's political and cultural history. Any 'hegemonic project' will be very much defined in Scottish terms. In the decade since the re-establishment of its parliament, Scotland has steadily diverged politically from England in several important respects.

In May 1999, the Parliament opened to a rendition of Burn's *A Man's a Man for a' That*. The message was clear. This would be a parliament for the ordinary man and woman – no Lords and Ladies, no medieval pomp and circumstance, no archaic flummery. The notion of common worth is powerfully inscribed in our culture. How this matches up with the reality of everyday life is, of course, another question – but myths are very real and influential in themselves. To its credit, the Parliament has developed as far more open and accessible to the people than its Westminster equivalent. There will be no second house in an independent Scotland. Our parliament is elected on the basis of proportional representation and it is fixed-term. Our expenses crisis – minor compared to the Westminster version – has been largely sorted out and the cynicism and disillusionment associated with Westminster politics is much less of a feature in Scotland. There is already a greater degree of popular control over government in Scotland than is the case in the UK. Coalition/minority governments are the norm.

The commitment to public services is very strong. The process of privatisation which has been such a striking feature of New Labour in England has no real equivalent in Scotland. The NHS is run by public Health Boards rather than Trusts; there has been no privatisation of GP practices; treatment centres remain under public control and the concept of patient choice and the internal market has not been promoted. The local authority comprehensive school remains the norm in Scotland while the percentage attending private schools is around half that in England. There will be no privately sponsored Academies nor will

Lib/Con plans to open 2,000 'free' schools on the Swedish model be taken up in Scotland. Scottish Water is publicly owned. A quarter of Scotland's workforce is employed in the public sector.

Writing in *The Red Paper on Scotland* in 1975, Jim Sillars wrote: *Land ownership has always aroused much stronger feelings in Scotland than any other part of the United Kingdom*[7]. There is a strong belief that the land should belong to those who work it. There are currently 34 major community land ownership schemes covering 1.4m acres. Most recently – Feb 2010 – the people of north Bute have voted overwhelmingly to purchase the estate owned by Richard Attenborough. There have never been trespass laws in Scotland and in 2003 the Parliament passed the Land Reform (Scotland) Act enshrining the freedom to roam across the private estates.

Eric Hobsbawm has no need to worry – Scotland has no intention of waging wars on anyone. Opposition to the war in Iraq, to nuclear weapons, to the Faslane submarine base all point to a very different foreign policy for an independent Scotland.

Immigration is not, nor ever has been, the highly emotive issue it is in England. The Parliament has a policy of welcoming immigrants as a counter to what has been a declining population. There are no indigenous xenophobic, right-wing, parties in Scotland able to whip up strong feelings around immigration. A recent attempt by the *'Scottish'*

---

[7] Jim Sillars: *Land Ownership and Land Nationalisation* in *Red Paper on Scotland*: EUSPB Edinburgh 1975

*Defence League* to hold a demonstration in Edinburgh was a total failure with a handful of members, mainly bussed up from England, totally swamped by a large anti-racist demonstration. There was also an interesting contrast between the UK leader's election debates and the Scottish equivalent in Edinburgh where all the comments coming both from the platform and from the floor were pro-immigrant.

Scotland is probably more pro-European Union than England. Among those supporting independence there is awareness that it would be essential for a small nation like Scotland to be part of Europe – as expressed in the SNP slogan *Independence in Europe.*

Scotland has an enlightened Criminal Justice record in relation to young people dating back to the Kilbrandon report of 1964 which led to the establishment of the Children's Hearing system in 1971 with the aim of decriminalising young offenders. In the words of the Scottish Government's statement on *Restorative Justice* published in 2008: *The fundamental difference between the children's hearings system and other youth justice systems is that by virtue of being referred to the reporter a child charged with an offence is diverted from prosecution in a criminal process and instead enters a non-retributive civil procedure which aims to meet the child's educational and developmental needs.*

Scotland has set itself ambitious targets in relation to reducing carbon emissions; 50% by 2030 and 80% by 2050. This compares to the UK government target of 60% by 2060 but, unlike the UK, the Scottish aims include aviation and shipping and do not depend on carbon trading. In line with the UK government, Scotland aims to generate 20% of energy from renewables by 2020 but in Scotland, significant progress has already been achieved – currently about 25% of our electricity is from renewable sources[8]. In March 2010, the Crown Estate leased 10 offshore sites to generate 1.2GW of electricity from wave and wind power. With 25% of Europe's potential wind and water energy, Scotland is well placed to rank as a world leader in relation to combating climate change.

This is a far from exhaustive list and it conveniently ignores lots of negatives. Similar audits of 'political positives' could be drawn up for England, Wales and Northern Ireland and each would be significantly different.

## The Political Left in Scotland

### The Scottish National Party

The political centre of gravity in Scotland remains broadly left of centre. Not only is the Scottish National Party, by its own definition, a social democratic, centre-left party, it is actually in power. In addition, the SNP is the largest party in local government with 363 council seats. In the 2009 European elections it polled 100,000 votes more than Labour and holds 2 of the 6 Scottish seats. At the SNP 2010 spring conference, Alex Salmond outlined what would be his demands in the event of a 'balanced' UK parliament including:

---

[8] Jenny Hogan, Director of Scottish Renewables. Letter in Herald. 1/4/10

- Saving £100m by scrapping House of Lords
- £5b by scrapping ID cards
- £100m by scrapping Trident
- £10m by scrapping the Scottish Office

The SNP's left credentials are usually judged in terms of its claim to be a social democratic party with its demand for independence being perceived either as not relevant or, more often, incompatible with left politics. However, in my opinion, it is *precisely* the demand for independence that most clearly defines the SNP as being on the left. I think there has been a tendency for the traditional left to assume ownership of left politics. We are delighted when organisations such as the SNP and the Greens 'come round to our way of thinking'. But left politics are in a state of flux. 'Our way of thinking' is being challenged once again by new social movements – just as it was by gender politics in the 1970s. *Liberté, égalité, fraternité* remain the cornerstones of left politics but how these concepts are interpreted changes from one historical epoch to another. In place of the strongly statist, economistic, and collectivist mind frame of the post-war epoch we require a new politics that combines both collectivism and individualism and is based on empowerment, pluralism and self realisation. As Roberto Unger puts it, we need to move on from the limited and conservative 'redistributive egalitarianism' of social democracy to a project which is about 'democratisation of the market, deepening of democracy and the empowerment of the individual'[9]. The central aim

---

[9] Robert Unger. *What the Left should Propose.* Verso. 2005

16

of the left must be nothing less than the radical democratic transformation of society with the concept of subsidiarity a key guiding principle; that all public institutions should be run at the lowest, least centralised level of society compatible with basic efficiency.

For the Scottish left, the transfer of state power from London to Edinburgh must be the *sine qua non* of any strategy of democratic transformation. But it is also of importance for left politics across the UK insofar as the secession of Scotland would put an end to the British state as it has existed for 300 years and would open the door to structural reform.

The SNP does have other left credentials – its opposition to the privatisation of our social services, to PFIs, to nuclear weapons and to the Iraq war. It has also set ambitious aims for the reduction of carbon emissions and has declared the aim of making Scotland a world leader in terms of renewable energy. It has recently launched an experiment whereby all Health Boards will have a majority of elected representatives. But perhaps the most impressive feature of the present SNP administration has been its enlightened approach to crime and punishment – always a key left-right indicator. Probably most memorable was its brave decision to release Mohmed Al Megrahi in the teeth of opposition from Scottish Labour and the US government. Scotland has one of the highest rates of imprisonment in Europe and the Prisons Commission which reported in Feb 2008 has set the aim of reducing the prison population by one third over ten years based on shifting the focus from punishment to pay-back. A high profile panel established by *Action for Children* has recently recommended extending the Children's Hearing system to cover 16 and 17 year olds[10] and the Scottish Government has set up a pilot scheme to divert the majority of young offenders away from the justice system altogether by offering intensive support programmes.

The SNP's main political weakness, however, lies in its approach to the financial and banking system. Alex Salmond has been widely criticised for his support for the 'arc of prosperity' – Norway, Denmark, Ireland, Iceland and Finland – and in particular his identification with the 'Celtic Tiger' economy. The government's economic policy has been very much a variant of the neo-liberal 'Washington consensus' with a focus on a low tax, low-regulation, business-friendly approach. Jim and Margaret Cuthbert have characterised the strategy as 'neo-liberalism with a heart'[11]. While it is now clear that this 'consensus' has collapsed, the SNP government has been slow to articulate a new economic vision for an independent Scotland. There is general agreement that any significant reform must include (i) the break-up of the large banks and (ii) the separation of retail and investment banking. However during a televised pre-election economy debate, Stewart Hosie, representing the SNP, made it quite clear the party

---

[10] Scottish Government: *Restorative Justice Services - for children and young people and those harmed by their behaviour* June 2008

[11] Jim Cuthbert and Margaret Cuthbert: *SNP Economic Strategy: Neo-liberalism with a Heart* in Gerry Hassan (ed) *The Modern SNP: from Protest to Power* Edinburgh University Press. 2009

did not support such reforms[12] – the one point of agreement between him and Labour's then Scottish Secretary, Jim Murphy. The restructuring and reform of the Royal Bank of Scotland is central to Scotland's economic future but for all of Scotland's political parties it remains the elephant in the room that no-one wants to talk about. It is crucial that the left engage with the SNP in the complex task of putting together an alternative strategy. There can be no return to Celtic tiger thinking and nor is there any convenient template available among the Nordic nations. The post-crash strategy will have to break new ground. What is certain is that without full fiscal autonomy at least, no such development is feasible.

## The Scottish Green Party.

The Green Party, with two Green MSPs, has an important contribution to make to the renewal of left politics in Scotland. Its 2007 Scottish election manifesto provides a detailed programme for the greening of the Scottish economy ranging from central policy down to a wide range of local and community initiatives and even further down to the concept of 'individual domestic tradable carbon quotas'. It can claim considerable credit in terms of influencing the government in the priority it is giving to renewable energy. In its 2010 election manifesto, it clearly calls for the 'mega-banks' to be broken up, for the separation of retail and investment banking and for a Tobin tax on all international financial transactions.

---

[12] *The Big Economy Debate*. Hosted by Glen Campbell. 10.24pm on April 25th 2010. BBC1

The concept of subsidiarity and local empowerment is very central to Green politics and serves to redress the historical failure of the left in relation to the devolution of power. Scottish Greens also have progressive policies on education, housing and the social services as well as being closely allied to the government on issues of crime and punishment. They also support the concept of a 'citizen's income' to replace our increasingly outdated benefit system and this is a concept which is likely to become of central importance in left thinking as the Tories dismantle the welfare state. The Greens put small and medium sized companies at the heart of their economic strategy and support experiments in mutualisation and co-operatives. The old left was almost exclusively urban in orientation. The Greens join the SNP and the Scottish Socialist Party in beginning to develop strategies for the countryside in general and farming, crofting and forestry in particular.

A further important feature of the new politics is their rejection of GDP and constant economic growth as a valid measure of a society's progress. At the heart of any 'green new deal' will be the concept of a sustainable, steady-state economy with the emphasis on the quality of life rather than simply consumption. This also challenges the traditional view that inequality can be resolved mainly through wealth redistribution, an economistic approach which has clearly not delivered equality. Andrew Sayer[13] convincingly argues that we need to focus much more on contributive rather than distributive justice.

---

[13] Andrew Sayer: *The Injustice of Unequal Work.* **Soundings** (43) Winter 2009, p. 102

Unskilled, mindless, repetitive, low status work has a profoundly negative impact on the workers involved and also on their families and feeds status and power inequality in society. The problem is we have evolved what is virtually a caste system as far as work is concerned. He argues on two fronts. Firstly unskilled work should be shared out. I work as an Educational Psychologist in a busy office. When I go home at night, cleaners come in and clear up after me. Why? Much of the filing, mailing, phone-answering is done by admin staff. All of these tasks are part and parcel of my job as a Psychologist and should be shared among us. But what would then happen to the admin and cleaning staff? Sayer coins the term 'hoarding' to describe the process whereby workers in high quality jobs seal off access to their professions. Access to my profession requires a university degree, post graduate training, and membership of the Health Professions Council as a pre-requisite to practice. But why can't non-qualified people, who show interest and aptitude, become apprentice psychologists and learn on the job. Qualifications and training would then follow as an enhancement rather than a precondition. The concept of equality is central to left politics and urgently requires updating. Michael Walzer[14] argues we need to abandon the idea of 'simple equality' with its implication of a common denominator, in favour of 'complex equality where social assets are fairly distributed but not equally possessed by every individual' – a pluralist equality. I think these

[14] Michael Walzer *Spheres of Justice*. Basic Books. New York, 1983

issues will prove to be very central to the new politics of the left.

The Greens also make important proposals for reform of the European Union. They argue for democratic reform giving the Parliament greater power over the Commission as well as a range of demands to promote equality, minimum wage protection, a 42 hour working week limit, an end to the dumping of EU products on developing countries together with fair trade deals, reform of the World Trade Organisation, an end to militarisation of the EU, a Tobin tax on financial transactions together with stronger regulation of banking.

This is very relevant to the argument presented by John Grahl that over the past decade or so, 'economic Europe' has increasingly taken precedence over 'social Europe'[15]. Centrally driven, legally enforceable, market integration based on the 'four freedoms' for corporations – rights to move goods, services, capital and labour anywhere without let or hindrance – has seriously undermined social rights. The 'European Social Model' has been systematically undermined and responsibility devolved to nation states. The consequence has been a race to the bottom with member states competing to attract investment and employment by cutting corporate tax, deregulating business practice and making labour markets and employment law as 'flexible' as possible. The inclusion of new member states formerly in the Soviet bloc has greatly widened inequality within

---

[15] John Grahl: *A Dead end for the EU.* **Soundings** Summer 2008

the Union but whereas, at an earlier post Maastricht phase, the challenge would have been to implement a programme of equalisation through positive social funding, the Lisbon approach has been to allow corporations to exploit the new arrivals. Globalisation, as presently constituted, represents a victory for finance capital and multi-national corporations over nation states freeing them up from political control and accountability; the consequence has been the most profound economic and social crisis for the Euro-zone in its history.

The left across Europe needs to come together to agree a long term strategy to create a democratic, sustainable, pluralist global economy. The immediate challenge is to rebalance market liberalisation with action to build a social Europe which regulates and shapes markets in the public interest, which protects and promotes the interests of developing economies and which works towards the reduction of carbon emissions across the world. *Compass* has done the left a service in producing a detailed, thought provoking policy document outlining an integrated European Union and global strategy.[16]

A weakness in Green politics is an over emphasis on local empowerment and insufficient importance given to power at the centre. The Greens support independence but it only appeared on the second last page of their 24 page 2007 Scottish manifesto and they felt the need to immediately qualify their support by making it clear that they were opposed to *exchanging one centralised state with another*

---

[16] Compass Programme for Renewal. *A New Political Economy*. Lawrence & Wishart. 2006

and that their support for independence had nothing to do with *nationalistic fervour*. But Scotland is a nation, not a locality and state power is a pre-requisite for bringing about democratic renewal at all levels of Scottish society. In their 2010 manifesto, support for independence is not mentioned at all – merely support for a referendum on the subject – pointing to a further retreat on the issue. And while they call for the state ownership of postal services and the rail network, surprisingly, they make no mention of bringing the oil and energy companies under democratic control – surely fundamental to the protection of the environment.

## The Scottish Socialist Party.

The SSP won 6 seats in the 2003 Scottish elections but, following the (crazy) breakaway of Tommy Sheridan to form the Solidarity party, it failed to achieve representation in 2007.

For the SSP, independence would represent a step forward to the establishment of a Scottish socialist republic. An ambitious aim. However in their 2007 election manifesto – over 50 pages long – they do indeed present a well argued and quite detailed case for what such a society might look like. Their manifesto is certainly the most visionary of the Scottish political parties: and vision is something we badly need at the moment. The programme covers all the elements of the new politics and is a tribute to how far the left has moved over the past few decades. The SSP are strong on the issue of democratic renewal at all levels of Scottish society – local government, the NHS, education, farming and crofting, industry – but they are the only party which seriously addresses power at the centre. The party calls for North Sea Oil, railways, banks, pharmaceuticals, all aspects of energy production and the construction industry to be brought under greater public control.

Clearly, we are not now talking about old-style top-down nationalisation. But what should replace it? The main theoretical work on this crucial issue was undertaken by Paul Hirst in the early 1990s under the rubric *Associative Democracy.*[17] In relation to industrial democracy, he argues for new legislation (updating the 1977 Bullock Report of fond memory) covering corporate governance which would:

- Take steps to break up large companies where feasible – say above 1000 employees – into smaller units attending to core activities which would be regionally located;

- Require such companies to establish a two-tier board

- (i) a Supervisory Board comprising one-third shareholders, one-third employee representatives elected by secret ballot and one-third community representatives (ii) a Management Board for day to day running of business but answerable to the Supervisory Board and (iii) a Works Council charged with the co-determination of company policy;

- Grant life-time employment contracts to all full-time employees with more than two years service along with single employee

[17] Paul Hirst: *Associative Democracy.* Polity Press. 1995

status with the same holidays, pension rights, terms of service and social facilities – the Japanese model;

- Part-time employees to be granted similar rights if they have worked for more than 16 hours a week for two years

- Require a 60% majority on the Supervisory Board for new share issues and mergers;

- *Employee Share Ownership Schemes* to be made available to employees – as per John Lewis's.

Good work has already been started in Scotland on this question – mainly by *Scottish Left Review* publications. Andy Cumbers[18]has tackled the daunting task of designing a structure which would bring Scotland's energy resources into full public ownership – very much in the spirit of Hirst's model:

- The 'supervisory' body would take the form of a Scottish Energy Agency (SEA) comprising one-third ministerial appointees, one-third local authority representatives and one-third employee representatives. This body would oversee the sector and set key objectives and targets. It would also oversee North Sea oil and gas developments;

- Oil and gas companies would be incorporated into a subsidiary organisation, the Scottish Hydrocarbons Corporation

[18] Andy Cumbers: *Economic Democracy and Public Ownership.* In *Reclaiming the Economy.* Scottish Left Review Publications. 2007

comprising two thirds nominated by the SEA and one third employee representatives;

- The electrical distribution companies – e.g. Scottish Power and Scottish Nuclear would be incorporated into the Scottish Energy Corporation with one-third SEA representatives, one-third consumer representatives and one-third employees

- Finally, a Scottish Renewables Association would be formed in which local authorities would have a 50% voice. Its main role would be to resource and co-ordinate the shift to renewable energy and would be comprised of local energy companies which would take a variety of forms.

OK, we are some distance away from implementing such a strategy, but it is essential for the left to explore new forms of democratic control appropriate for the different component parts of our economy.

The main weakness in the SSP programme is its rather 'old labour' attitude to the European Union. On the one hand, it calls for far reaching reform of the World Trade Organisation and the World Bank but on the other it supports a further referendum on our membership of the European Union. It loosely aligns itself with the anti-global movement (which has rather run out of steam) and is also part of the *European Anti-Capitalist Left* made up of a dozen or so small European socialist parties. But Europe is the power bloc through which we must operate to have any hope of making a difference at global level.

## The Scottish Labour Party

Since 1997, the Scottish Labour Party (SLP) has loyally supported every New Labour initiative – including the war in Iraq and the renewal of Trident. In particular the SLP has adopted a populist, authoritarian stance on law and order calling for compulsory prison sentences for anyone caught carrying a knife – something not even the UK Labour has called for. During the Thatcher years, Scotland's Labour MPs were dubbed 'the feeble 50' and thirty years later things have not materially changed – not one of the contingent of 38 MPs in the last UK parliament could be described as being on the left of the Party. While there are left elements within the Party grouped around the Campaign for Socialism, only 5 out of 46 Labour MSPs are listed as members.

However, difficult decisions are going to have to be faced. UK Labour is almost certain to construct its opposition to the Lib-Con government around a contest for the centre ground within which resistance to cuts and job losses is likely to be fairly muted. For the first time in many years, there will be no Scots in the leading positions in the UK Party. So it is possible that the SLP will begin to distance itself from London Labour and seek to present itself as Scotland's defender against Tory cuts. The difficulty is that such a strategy would require the Party to join a broad coalition of forces arguing for additional powers for the Scottish Parliament. That would mean allying itself, to some extent at least, with the SNP and that remains totally anathema to Scottish Labour. My guess is that they will be unable to construct a coherent, thought-out strategy adequate to address

28

the new circumstances they face and will opt for muddling through. They firmly believe that they have a divine right to rule Scotland and so thinking has never really been required. It will take a second defeat by the SNP to force Scottish Labour to face reality.

## *Prospects*

This Tory dominated coalition government will use the recession to drastically reduce spending on public services through cut-backs and privatization – starting with Royal Mail. The economic strategy is clear: the mass of the British people will bear the economic and social cost of restoring the fortunes of the City of London. Scotland's public sector is proportionately larger than England's so the consequences north of the border could be extremely serious – which is why Scotland voted overwhelmingly against the return of a Tory government. But that vote will count for little. The UK government will simply slash Scotland's block grant and Holyrood's role will be reduced to one of managing cuts.

The future of the Scottish left will largely be determined by how we respond to this challenge. Two options should be considered.

Firstly, there is what could be described as the unionist option. This option accepts that the British people have elected a government committed to an economic model which views expenditure on public services as an expensive luxury we can now ill afford. So, yes, Scotland will have to accept the verdict of the electorate and shoulder its 'fair share' of the pain. However, there is, perhaps, room to argue that Scotland should be given special dispensation on a range of grounds – its high levels of deprivation, our current 'dependency' on the public sector, the expense of servicing sparsely populated areas and so on. The perspective would be to work for the return of a Labour government to Westminster which would hopefully undo most of the damage. This will probably be the response of Scottish Labour. The trouble is the strategy is unlikely to work. There is already a growing perception in England that Scotland has been getting unfair preferential treatment for years and that it is time it we paid a more equal share – in 2006/7 expenditure per capita was 20% higher in Scotland than England. The new government has already initiated a 'needs assessment' review of the Barnett formula; so Scotland could face a double whammy – a 'fair share' of the cuts on top of a drastically reduced block grant.

The truth is there is no longer a unionist answer to the challenge we face. For possibly the first time since the establishment of the Scottish parliament, the economic model is right at the centre of the debate. The social democratic settlement which has bound Scotland and England together for half a century is well and truly over. It's make your mind up time for Scotland. Accepting a UK neo-liberal cure for the recession, geared to the needs of the south east of England, will do incalculable damage to Scotland's economic and social infrastructure. The Scottish people clearly voted for something different and that aspiration should be respected and acted upon. The challenge for the left in Scotland is to articulate an alternative vision of a sustainable, social economy which gives priority to high quality public services and which reflects

Scottish values and priorities. Any such perspective will demand full control of our economy – not least because North Sea oil revenues will be an important component part.

This radical option requires a left committed to independence or, as a minimum, devolution-max. Effective joint working between the 'unionist' and 'self-government' lefts will, in my view, become increasingly problematic as time goes by; the constitution has become a watershed issue. As things stand, it looks like Scotland's version of the 'progressive political alliance' will be built around the SNP, the Greens, the SSP and sections of the trade union movement.

Finally, it should be noted that the Scottish left is well served by two networking/policy groupings, the *Scottish Democratic Left* (SDL) and, already mentioned, the *Scottish Left Review* (SLR). Both publish magazines – *Perspectives* and *Scottish Left Review* – exploring the terrain of left renewal. DLS and SLR have an important role to play in generating the ideas around which the new vision for Scotland can be constructed as well as promoting debate across social and political agencies.

# Left Out: Policies for a Left Opposition

# An Economic Strategy for the Left

## Peter Lawrence

### The Crisis

The world in the grip of another crisis of what we still like to call capitalism. The financial crisis of 2007-8 coincided with, and contributed to a major recession, which has now brought the Greek economy to its knees and the integrity of the Eurozone, barely a decade into its existence, seriously challenged by speculators in the global financial markets. At least a third of the world's population 'lives' on purchasing power parity incomes of $1.25 a day or lower. There are increasing inequalities both within and between countries. Wars continue to be fought in various parts of the world at different times, though this decade has been dominated by war in Iraq and the continuing battles in Afghanistan. In various parts of the 'developing' world, there are variously civil wars, unstable governments and rule by warlords, sometimes in a combination of all three. There is a global crisis of the environment which does not look as though it will be taken seriously enough by a sufficient number of countries to be averted.

But it is the economic and financial crisis which takes centre stage. For the Left, the challenge is to forge an economic strategy that deals with the short term aspects of the current crisis as part of a process to effect a longer run shift towards a socialist economy, namely an economy that is collectively organised and democratically accountable. The emergence of the UK's first coalition government since the second world war with a clear economic programme embedded in the neo-liberal economic orthodoxy offers the opportunity for the Left to mobilise opposition to this programme around a robust alternative which connects to the principles of cooperation and mutuality that are at the root of a socialist economy and society while exercising appropriate care and responsibility with public finances. This essay seeks to map out such a strategy.

In the UK 2010 election the choice between the three main parties revolved around reducing the fiscal deficit: the speed at which public expenditure cuts should be made and the nature of the tax increases, and tax structure, needed to increase revenue. Cutting the budget deficit sharply over a relatively short period of time would, it was argued by the Conservatives, keep interest rates low, thus encouraging private instead of public investment, with consequent growth of economic activity and of employment. It was argued that doing nothing about the budget deficit and accumulating public debt would make that debt more expensive to service as the increasingly international lenders would demand higher interest rates. Higher debt repayment would also have an adverse effect on the budget deficit. Labour's policy (and incidentally that of the IMF) was to delay cuts until 2011-12 but Labour undertook then to halve the structural deficit within four years. The Liberal Democrats also embraced delaying the cuts. We shall return to these arguments below.

The new coalition government has adopted the Conservative policy of starting cuts now with a £6 billion net cut in expenditure to be followed by much bigger cuts to be made in 2011-12. Together with similar policies being followed by governments across Europe, most aggressively in Ireland and Greece, it is almost inevitable that there will be at best a very slow recovery with an inevitable increase in unemployment and at worst the possibility of a double dip recession, both prospects further inducing a reluctance to invest, thus creating a self-fulfilling deeper recession bordering on depression, or at best a period of stagnation. The latest inflation figure may also be putting pressure on the new Government to reduce the budget deficit quickly, although the Bank of England seems clear that current inflation running at 3.7% is a temporary phenomenon driven by rising oil prices, sterling depreciation (which worsens the effect of the increase in the US dollar denominated oil prices) and the restoration of the 17.5% rate of VAT. (When these factors are stripped out, inflation falls to 1.4%, well within the targeted range). 'Quantitative easing' does not seem to have had much effect either for reasons mentioned below. There is no evidence either of wage increases fuelling inflation but plenty of evidence of pay freezes in operation. So for the moment, inflation is not an important part of the picture.

For a short while in the present crisis, there was an emerging belief that the 'system' needed serious reform and considerable interest in an alternative way of organising economic and social life, evident in the columns of newspapers and in the media generally. Even sales of Marx's *Capital* were reported to have increased in the wake of the financial and economic crisis which began in 2007.

Governments and economic commentators talked of reforming the banking system. Some governments actually nationalised banks, and the US government of both Bush and Obama nationalised some financial institutions and even aided the ailing auto industry. Almost all governments propped up consumption by pouring money into the economy to prevent a repeat of the Great Depression of the 1930s. As a result, most economies now have budget deficits which are considerably higher than the 3% standard by which economies had been governed until now. There has been a consequent increase in the size of the accumulated public debt to record post World War II levels. There has been much talk of a new kind of economic order in which markets and their products would be better regulated, executive salaries and bankers' bonuses would be capped, the rich would be taxed at higher rates and corporate governance would be reformed to encourage mutual organisations such as the building societies and the cooperative movement.

Very little of this talk has yet been transformed into action. In spite of the revulsion against the high CEO pay and bonuses of both the financial and industrial sectors, bank bonuses may be down but they are still being paid, while CEOs in both sectors are coming away with remuneration packages reportedly as high as £95 million in one year. Banks have seriously reduced their lending and preferred to use the cash created by 'quantitative easing' to bolster their asset position. The 'markets' which gave us credit default swaps and similar derivative products and have been rescued by governments are returning to their position of power and now determine the fate of

36

several economies in the Eurozone, if not of the currency itself. They also appear to be pressurising the UK and other governments into making premature cuts in their budget deficits. However, the coalition government has declared its intention to set up a commission to examine the issue of separating retail and investment banking, to introduce a banking levy, to deal with 'unacceptable bonuses', to give the Bank of England more regulatory power and to foster competition and mutuality in the banking system. The Government intends to put a cap on public sector pay though not one on the private sector.

There is also talk of addressing the underlying imbalance of the British economy with its shift from manufacturing, now only 12% of GDP, to services and especially financial services. The issue of inequality has briefly raised its head but only the Liberal Democrats have seriously talked about redistribution through changes in tax rates and structure and within the coalition, have succeeded in getting the policy of gradually raising the personal allowance to £10,000 over the next few years a move that will help the lower paid. However, the Child Trust Fund which turned out to be as very effective way of getting lower income families to save for their children's future is being scrapped thus likely to increase inequality in the long term.

The current situation is thus portrayed as a short term problem which can be resolved by the kinds of economic policies that have been pursued since the late 1970s – reducing the budget deficit and the size of the state, allowing markets to operate freely subject to a degree (perhaps now a greater degree) of regulation, keeping taxes low, privatising public services through sub-contracting and investment in new public sector capital expenditure through public-private partnerships. Yet it is precisely this package of policies, developed by the Conservative governments of 1979–1997 and the subsequent New Labour governments (and their counterparts across the world), that resulted in the economic and financial crisis of 2007-8 with all the consequences that have unfolded since. Where Labour had the opportunity to discard its slavish subservience to the City and big capital generally, this time with popular support, its credibility might have been shot because of that previous subservience. It is hard to believe the Conservatives will tackle their business friends other than to finance their party, while the Liberal Democrats have fallen in with the Conservative Party's liberal economics. However popular action against banks, bonuses and the corporate culture of greed would have been and still could be, politicians of all colours, possibly because now they know no other way, are still in thrall to the markets which are largely controlled by corporate financial and industrial capital.

Whether it is accurate to describe the crisis as simply the bursting of a bubble in financial markets or something more serious is an important issue in considering what is to be done. There is some evidence that the economic system was undergoing a periodic bout of over-production brought about by the credit-fuelled consumption boom in housing and durables. Part of the cause of the financial crisis was the beginnings of a recession which burst the housing bubble and caused the collapse of the derivatives markets in property debt. The interaction between the collapse of financial markets and the forecast recession in product markets then brought about a more substantial financial crisis which effectively transformed private debt into public. More seriously, these developments may have coincided with a low point in a longer economic cycle associated with a period when existing technologies cannot be developed further but before a major technological change generates a new period of growth. This unfortunate combination requires a strategy not only to overcome the immediate economic and financial crisis, not only to generate a longer term investment plan, but more crucially to identify from where a new technological revolution might emerge. In respect of this last area of debate, the hot money has been placed on a technological revolution based on 'green' technologies. Indeed it could be argued that this revolution in a technological sense, has already occurred and it is the production of the necessary machine tools and final products embodying this technology to which investment should be directed. There are also developments in biotechnology which could form the basis of a major technological leap where again investment may need to be channelled.

## *The Left's Alterative Economic Strategy in Retrospect*

Is there a Left alternative economic strategy which both addresses the short term issues and then looks forward well into the 2010s and beyond that can bring together the critiques of modern capitalism to generate a popular strategy movement for systemic change? To answer these questions, it is first worth looking at the previous ideas around Left alternative economic strategies. The notion of an

alternative economic strategy developed in the
1970s in a period of economic stagnation
culminating in the financial rescue package of the
IMF in 1976, a moment which marked the
beginning of the Chicago neo-liberal economic
strategy applied to the UK. For the Left an
alternative economic strategy at that time seemed
fairly straightforward. Emerging out a variety of
organised groups in the Labour Party and the trades
unions, the strategy was also associated with the
British Communist Party, which itself had
considerable influence on the left of the Labour
Party and on the unions. David Purdy[19], writing
after the Conservatives' 1979 election victory
describes the main version of the AES thus:

> *The TUC and some members of the Labour
> Left have tended to press for a programme of
> economic expansion, import controls, greater
> powers of intervention for the NEB[20] and
> planning agreements between the government
> and public and private companies, as the
> radical quid pro quo for pay restraint within
> the framework of a Social Contract between
> the Labour government and the TUC.*

Purdy noted the tension on the Left about pay
policy. In the late '60s and the whole of the 1970s,
governments had to grapple with rising inflation.
Pay policy became an important issue because the

19 David Purdy, *The Left's Alternative Economic Strategy*, **Politics and Power**, No 1,
1980

20 The National Enterprise Board was set up in 1975. It was intended to be the vehicle
by which the UK government would make strategic investments in key sectors of UK
manufacturing. One of its main functions came to be rescuing through public ownership
failed sections of manufacturing such as British Leyland and reviving them, something
that was successfully done in the case of Ferranti.

conventional wisdom was that rising inflation was a consequence of an increase in costs fuelled by wage increases. The third element in this process in the successful capitalist countries was productivity. UK productivity growth lagged behind those successful economies hence as wage rises ran ahead of productivity increases, unit costs of production rose and could only be covered by higher prices. If wage rises could be kept in line with productivity increases then prices would not need to rise. If prices did not rise, then wage claims seeking to maintain or even increase real wages would not be inflationary. The other side of the inflationary process was the situation of excess demand, allowing sellers to raise prices to bring demand in line with supply. This was less of a problem with membership of what became the EU as this opened up the UK to competing European producers, and would clearly be less of a problem with increased investment in UK companies in order to compete successfully in Europe, but would become an issue if import controls were to be imposed in order to protect revived UK manufacturing, at least in the short term.

Purdy's critique of the 1970s AES demonstrated a recognition, not generally accepted on the Left at the time, that capitalism had changed, but that the AES appeared to respond to a capitalism of the 1930s rather than to the changed capitalism of the 1970s in which the State has taken a prominent role not only in securing the welfare of its citizens through various social measures in health, social security and education, but also through substantially increased state direction of the economy to deal with the market failures of capitalism demonstrated in the 1930s.

Internationally the capitalist world economy was changing, too. Not only had the UK voted in a referendum to stay in a European common market, but the thrust of post-war international policies had been to reduce trade barriers. The GATT (now the WTO) rounds of negotiations were doing this, slowly and with many exceptions, but the main point was that nobody wanted to return to the protectionism of the 1930s which restricted trade and therefore output.

The AES emphasis on the need for State intervention in manufacturing enterprises to direct investment towards advanced technology and therefore higher productivity suggested, as Purdy wryly noted, a move to a centralised state socialism, of which the contemporary exemplars were not universally regarded as models of democratic socialism or successful economies. Indeed, in seeking to remedy the defects of British capitalism, it became unclear what was socialist about the AES. Restoring British competitiveness and reducing unemployment through State action would be a continuation of various attempts by Conservative and Labour governments, until 1979, to sustain capitalism. Purdy pointed out that the issue was not that more investment was required but what kind of investment it would be, to which sectors it would go, for which purposes it would be invested and what would be the expected consequences of such investment. His responses are worth quoting at length:

*A socialist investment policy would frame its answers to these questions on the basis of needs which find no expression in the market, or are currently met in ways distorted by privilege and oppression. Examples of such needs are the protection of the environment and the conservation of finite resources; the automation of routine, humdrum tasks and the enhancement of the quality of working life in general; progress towards the eventual abolition of the sexual division of labour by way of steps towards the socialisation of child care and housework and the expansion and adaptation of education and training facilities for women; resistance towards the division between mental and manual labour and the hierarchical and oppressive systems of authority and subordination that have been built on this division; the promotion of a balanced and equitable regional economic structure and the rehabilitation of inner city communities; the need to reduce the inequalities which divide the developed rich from the backward poor nations of the world.*

It would be wrong to say that no progress has been made towards achieving at least some of the goals, thought with many faltering steps. Environmental issues are high on the agenda and steps have been taken to reduce carbon emissions, both through the price mechanism and through changes in legislation which have lead to greater recycling and less pollution. The position of women has been improved with greater possibilities of beginning and sustaining a working life through greater nursery provision and tax concessions on workplace nurseries, the institution of still inadequate paternal and parental leave arrangements, as well as support for single mothers to gain employment. The wider provision of flexitime arrangements has further assisted this development. There has also been increased participation by women in education and training. The re-development of city and town centres as places to live as well as work has been quite striking, while attempts to shift parts of government and public sector organisations out to the regions has generated employment for these regions if not balanced regional economies.

However, while much change in these areas is evident, in other areas developments have worsened. Hierarchical forms of organisation have become more commonplace, especially in the public sector. The division between mental and manual labour is probably greater with the creation of more 'white-collar' jobs, especially in media and IT, shifting aspirations further away from skilled manual than ever before. There has been some attempt to reverse the virtual disappearance of apprenticeships and some effort to elevate the status of skilled and semi-skilled manual qualifications but such occupations are still considered of lower social status than the manual ones. As for the developing countries, the gap between the developed, and richer developing countries and the rest has been increasing, in spite of, or possibly because of the substantial intervention through humanitarian and development aid of international government organisations, individual governments and NGOs.

So there is much left to be done in pursuit of this particular socialist agenda. Purdy proposed an investment strategy which would need to be spearheaded by the State but which need not involve bureaucratic and centralised state controls, and could be popular without involving a major ideological shift:

> *Examples of such projects are investment in energy conservation and alternative renewable energy sources. For instance a programme of providing every publicly owed building with a solar heating panel and adequate insulation would bring much needed relief to the construction industry and would generate the usual multiplier effects on demand in the rest of the economy. The development of local authority district heating schemes would re-assert community interest in and control over the supply and use of energy. And if funds were committed by central government to research and development on renewable energy sources on anything approaching the scale of the nuclear power programme, it is probable that proven projects would emerge*

A similar paragraph could have been written today. And, as today, Purdy's proposals for a major investment in the railway network, democratic local planning for integrated transport, rapid urban transport, electric cars and improved provision for bicycles are highly topical, however many the steps that have been taken, especially since 1997, to improve public transport services and to provide the road connections for an integrated transport structure.

## *'Capitalism' Today*

However, if the 1970s was not the 1930s, the crisis of 2007-8 threatened to be much more like the 1930s and nothing like the 1970s. Moreover, it occurred when the world had changed arguably more since the 1970s than it had between the 1930s and 1970s. In particular, the globalisation of the world economy, fuelled by an unprecedented leap in communications technology and passenger travel and air freight, was accelerated by the parallel globalisation of financial services with trading in stocks and shares round the clock. Although globalisation was nothing new, and had been developing apace since the late 19th century, the increasing freedom of trade (already taken into account in Purdy's analysis and accelerated by the various rounds of the GATT, now WTO), together with almost unfettered capital mobility, facilitated the development of global corporations with the ability to move production around the world to where costs (usually, though not always, labour costs), were lowest. As a consequence pure national control over economic strategy is even less a feasible option than it was in the 1970s. For countries like the UK, now an integral part of a major economic bloc, having joined what is now the EU in 1973, it is inconceivable that either import or capital controls, two of the major features of the old alternative strategy, could be implemented. Even those countries that lie outside economic unions can no longer operate an economic strategy that goes contrary to the prevailing free trade orthodoxy except with special and very temporary dispensation.

What is certainly clear from the experience of the 20th century, as a whole. is that capitalism has proved to have greater resilience and dynamism in the face of its many, sometimes severe, crises than might have been expected by Marx and his comrades in the 19th century. It is not an original proposition to argue that the victories of the various social movements, most notably the trades unions, in shortening the working week, improving health and safety at work, increasing real take home pay and the share of wages in national income, providing access to almost free health care for everyone, widening access to the higher levels of education and eventually improving the position of those at the bottom of the heap with the minimum wage and various tax credits, have sown the seeds of capitalism's resilience where previously they had been expected to sow the seeds of capitalism's destruction. The idea of a working class led revolution to overthrow Capital is less credible now than it has ever been. The concessions forced out of Capital have resulted in a very different system from the one with which Marx grappled.

Modern capitalist economies are dominated by large enterprises, themselves the result of mergers and acquisitions both of other large enterprises and of smaller ones. Indeed it is worth asking the questions as to whether these economies are still capitalist in the sense of Marx and therefore whether we are in a transitional phase leading towards a more socially directed economic system that already contains some of the features of a potentially socialist economy and society as conceived by 19th and early 20th century Marxists. To be sure our economies are dominated by the power of capital, but the ownership of the dominant large private enterprises is heavily skewed towards other large enterprises with interlocking shareholdings between extractive, manufacturing and financial sectors (especially pension funds). Mr Moneybags is no longer the main character in the system in which capital accumulation is the main driving force of capitalist enterprise. Enterprises have to satisfy many different stakeholders. In other words the old idea that the objective of the firm is to maximise profits in order to re-invest and accumulate capital has been replaced by the profit maximisation objective subjected to a number of constraints, of which keeping employees, customers and shareholders happy, maintaining or increasing market share in order to maximise economies of scale, and investing in product research and development are just a few.

However, in spite of the increasing impersonalisation of capital, it is still the case that power over capital is increasingly concentrated in a relatively few global financial and industrial enterprises whose survival as successful and sustained organisations is superintended by very powerful and highly paid individuals whose own personal interests as well as reputations depend to a great extent on the success of the enterprise. In the current crisis it is clear that it is these individuals that have the greatest influence over market sentiment and government policy. These developments in the organisation of capital have been matched by a great stratification of labour, and especially in the UK, a low level of social mobility which has solidified these strata into well-defined social classes. This has undermined working class solidarity, reduced the appeal and power of organised labour, and increasingly individualised what was once a collectively conscious social and economic force. Supported by the prevailing economic theories of the last four decades, the notion of a collective social consciousness underpinned by mutual interdependence of individuals has been replaced by notions of the maximisation of individual utility in competition with others. All this has occurred paradoxically during an era in which there has been an expansion of the kind of voluntary activity and charitable appeals both nationally and internationally in which a sense of altruism and of community is dominant.

## *A 21st Century Left Alternative Economic Strategy?*

A discussion of an alternative strategy for the Left needs to consider short term policies to deal with the immediate economic situation and then a medium to long run strategy which presents the distinctly democratic collectivist approach to economic strategy which distinguishes a socialist strategy from a simply State interventionist one. The most immediate economic issue is that of the budget deficit. It is clear that the major contribution to the increased deficit is the fiscal stimulus that Labour applied to the economy in the wake of the 6% fall in GDP following the financial crisis. That fall in GDP itself contributed to a decline in tax revenues which added to the further decline in revenues following the temporary VAT cut. Part of the fiscal stimulus involved increases in government expenditure, for example the vehicle scrappage scheme, that had some effect in propping up consumer demand and preventing the economy from going into meltdown, and, as unemployment increased, expenditure on benefits. It is therefore argued that as the economy recovers, tax revenues will rise, unemployment expenditure will fall and the budget deficit will shrink. However, this 'automatic stabiliser' effect of budget deficits will only deal with one part of the deficit. A return of revenues and expenditure to its levels prior to the crisis still leaves a 'structural' deficit, estimated by the Institute of Fiscal Studies at £90bn, though this figure may actually be nearer £80bn, which after the recent downward estimate of the 2009-10 deficit to £156bn would be around 6% of GDP. There is also a substantial saving that could be made by reducing our military commitments to a level consistent with our economic status. The Liberal Democrats were not in favour of renewing Trident, while a substantial part of the population running across the political spectrum questions the UK participation in the war in Afghanistan. These are important political issues which have economic consequences and around which a 'joined-up' Left political and economic strategy could emerge.

Over the short term, such annual deficits are added to the national debt which now also includes the money spent on bailing out the banks. In the longer run such annual additions are unsustainable, because they require increasing amounts of current expenditure to service the debt and because they are potentially inflationary. Therefore a plan is required to effect a reduction in these annual additions to the National Debt. The Coalition seeks to reduce the annual deficit sharply so that at the end of its five year period of office the deficit will be at the magic 3% of GDP and it intends to do this by laying much greater emphasis on expenditure cuts than tax increases. However, in the present situation where the private sector is not investing or is unable to invest because of a combination of uncertainty, signs of lower consumer spending and a caution on the part of the banks to lend money, it would seem wiser to put the emphasis on maintaining as much public investment expenditure as possible even if this has to be financed by increases in taxation. This will mean a slower rate of reduction of the budget deficit but is preferable to a faster rate which stunts recovery. This may increase total national debt but if, as is very likely, the nationalised banks are sold off at a profit, national debt will be correspondingly reduced at a greater rate than anticipated, thus leaving room for more flexibility in the rate of reduction of the budget deficit. The term over which the deficit is reduced could be doubled or trebled as part of a 10 or 15 year plan to regenerate a different kind of economy.

An alternative to public investment is to direct the state-owned banks to increase lending to the private sector rather than give priority to restoring their capital asset adequacy position. If the banks did not do this but, as it seems to have been the case, increased their profits, then a windfall tax on bank profits which is channelled into a government sponsored lending scheme would be an obvious option. Further, if private investment is sluggish because of uncertainty about the future, government investment through such a bank-taxation mechanism offers the chance of developing a range of infrastructural programmes that would improve the prospects for inward private investment, improve the quality of life, increase employment possibilities and stimulate the location of green technology enterprise in the UK.

Such government investment could be also financed by an increase in general taxation as households reduce their expenditure. A higher tax allowance for low incomes, the restoration of the 10% band and a more progressive structure that not only taxes incomes of more than £150k at 50% but of more than £250k at 60%, and has intervening bands at 30 and 40% would be a fairer way of distributing the household sacrifices. Most importantly, if these raised revenues are directed towards investment they will increase employment opportunities and have the multiplier effects which will maintain other areas of employment and thus maintain both investment and consumption oriented economic activity. Even with the existing tax structure, a one percentage point on the standard rate of tax would raise £5.5bn in a full year, and on the higher rate £1.8bn. A two or three percentage point increase would make serious inroads into the budget deficit and with a slower rate of deficit reduction allow room for investment expenditure to generate growth and employment. This is preferable to an increase in the essentially regressive VAT and a principled Left position should oppose increases in VAT as the undoubtedly favoured tax measure of the Conservative led coalition. Putting the emphasis on reducing consumption and increase investment in producer goods would also shift the economy away from reliance on growth through continuous rises in personal consumption inevitably stimulated by credit growth and leading to another crisis.

The above short and medium run economic strategy is well within the bounds of the macro-economic management of a capitalist economy and is a necessary but not sufficient element of a clearly socialist strategy. So what specifically could comprise a progressive and distinctly socialist investment strategy? An environmental sustainability strategy of, for example, putting solar panels on every roof for heating water and for generating electricity, installing wind turbines for community electricity generation or individual turbines for every building, and of wall and roof insulation and double glazing for every building, would all reduce considerably carbon emissions, reduce the energy bills of households and businesses as well as local and central government, and create employment for both skilled and unskilled workers. A programme of housing refurbishment, especially of derelict and abandoned properties, could also reduce the degree to which the housing problem is addressed through greater green belt incursion. Investment in the rail network, with emphasis on creating transport hubs at airports and in the centre of towns and cities, on introducing urban trams across the country and expanding the very successful existing networks, and on upgrading cross country rail routes, would generate a boost to the construction industry. Creating motorway-side coach parks to speed up coach travel and reduce the number of cars on motorways would also help reach the carbon emission targets. Investment in R&D for electric powered transport and more energy extensive cars and other vehicles would also make a contribution to reducing reliance on non-renewables as well as building up a green technology capability. Better road maintenance and increasing promotion of safe cycling would help meet both carbon emission and public health targets.

The market will not do this, though such a programme will create much commercial market activity. Such a programme will require a large amount of public borrowing, though people might be persuaded to pay higher taxes in the short run to achieve lower energy bills two or three years down the line. Increases in fuel and road tax, coupled with wider application of congestion charges and the introduction of road pricing could help finance green transport investment. What is certain is that the prevailing view that public expenditure needs to be reined in to reduce the budget deficit will not produce the programme outlined above. Therefore a strategy which seeks to exercise greater control over market forces and to push economies and societies in a more collectivist direction has to be an international one in at least the issue of regulation of markets and large capital, although countries have a lot to learn from each other in the promotion of more collective forms of organisation and decision making in the economic and social spheres.

A shift towards more collective ways of operation requires a change in the strategy towards corporate control. The mainstream Left, and especially the trades unions, have always taken an ambivalent attitude towards industrial democracy. Trades unions have regarded proposals for employee representation on company boards of directors as compromising their bargaining power. Yet part of the problem with industrial relations is inadequate information about the performance of enterprises. Having employee representation on corporate boards of directors could be a first step in worker participation and a greater degree of employee control over company decision making. Such representation would have to reflect the different categories of employee and would require training in understanding accounts and all aspects of company business. Closer knowledge of the company's financial position and prospects for the future would enable realistic pay deals to be concluded and especially help to curb the excesses of executive salaries. For this development to be acceptable to the Left, there would have to be a recognition of the changed character of capitalism and the fact that under large scale corporate capitalism, everyone is an employee selling their labour power to the organisation that employs them.

Such developments, and they could be reproduced in the public sector organisations, whether local authorities, government departments or publically owned companies, could also be a way of reducing the disparities in income which have been generated over the last 30 years. Although people at the bottom of the income distribution have improved their position in recent years, at least in the UK, a relatively small section of the population with higher incomes have steamed ahead. In the UK, over 90% of the population earns less than £50,000 a year, while the CEO of Reckitt Benckiser took home £93 million in salary, bonuses and share options in 2009. A remuneration committee consisting of different groups of employees as well as senior management, might take a different view about the appropriate rewards for a CEO, than a committee composed entirely of executive and non-executive directors. The adoption of Drucker's maximum ratio of 20:1 for top to bottom salaries would be a good start.

Industrial democracy is one step forward towards developing new ownership forms which reduce the concentration of control over long term decision making in both public and private sectors. The promotion of employee share ownership may be the appropriate place to start given where we are. This could start with a stipulation that some percentage of shares in a company would be held by employees for the duration of their employment and could only be sold when their employment ended. The mutualisation of production enterprises in which ownership is vested in the employees with equal voting rights would be another option. Mutualisation of retailing based on the Cooperative model could spread to other retail organizations. The Labour Party's promotion in its manifesto of supporter owned football clubs need not stop at football, and the Left should take this opportunity of building on this currently popular approach to ownership.

If the coalition government can advance mutualisation of financial institutions in its programme, there is no reason why the Left cannot push this further by advocating the mutual model for all financial institutions.

So, last but not least, we turn to the financial sector. In the short term, the issues associated with the financial crash need to be addressed. Breaking up the banks into investment and retail arms is opposed by the industry but is surely necessary even if it reduces bank profits and sources of credit. Alongside these changes would be changes in the regulation of financial institutions and their products and in particular a requirement for new financial products to be licensed before they can be traded on the markets. More longer run reforms would involve reconversion to mutuals of those banks that were originally building societies and promotion of credit unions and other smaller localised forms of mutuality to channel credit to lower income groups. These moves would not preclude various forms of industrial democracy for the employees of the mutuals as well as a share in the ownership of these institutions with customers.

## Conclusions

A Left alternative strategy needs to comprise four main elements.

First it requires an analysis of the development of modern capitalism that recognizes the degree to which key elements of that system have changed and made redundant many of the central tenets of previous left alternatives and identify a strategy which builds a left alternative out of those elements of the economic system that move economic activity and organization in a collectivist direction.

Secondly, it requires a set of policies for the immediate resolution of the financial and economic crisis.

Thirdly it requires a longer term strategy that is based on the need for more democratic collectivist solutions. A strategy that incorporates redistribution, regulation, publically led investment in an environmentally sustainable set of new technologies, mutuality, industrial democracy and more cooperative forms of ownership, would not only be popular but would also renew the sowing of the sends of a progressive and democratic socialist society whose construction was the original purpose of the Left.

Finally any strategy has to be internationally orientated. On the issues of financial regulation, the environment and the coordination of economic policy, it is clear that national solutions can only be partial and that international cooperation is essential. In the wake of the current crisis, greater international cooperation has been evident as has greater coordination of policy whether via the IMF or the EU and other economic groupings. Cooperation between the political forces of the Left around the world with a common economic and political position is an essential part of moving not just the UK but the world economy in that progressive socialist direction.

## Labour's 'Critical Friends': Compass, the Labour left and the CPGB

## Andrew Pearmain

> *"All I've been doing the last few years is go back to stuff I was reading twenty years ago, and realizing its relevance,"* Neal Lawson, Compass chairperson (personal interview)

The Labour left has always occupied an oddly indeterminate position in British politics. Neither wholly of the left nor entirely within the Labour Party, it has tended to combine the worst of both worlds, and not to be taken seriously in either. Burdened with the historical associations of leftism (dogmatism and fanaticism, and basic fealty to the Soviet Union) and of Labourism (ultimate reliance on the trade unions, and a narrow focus on electoralism and parliamentarism), it has always had to operate on political terms set by others. It has had its moments of noisy ascendancy – Labour revulsion at MacDonald's 1930s betrayals, Bevan in the 1950s, the Campaign for Labour Party Democracy and Benn's deputy leadership campaign in the early 1980s – but has never exercised sustained influence over the politics of the Labour Party, let alone serious power in the government of the country.

Right now, it's hard to even identify a left wing within the Labour Party. Its most strident expression, the self-styled 'Labour Representation Committee', is little known and even less effective; a kind of Bennite hard left 'friends re-united', or

GLC glory days re-enactment society. It only seems to spring to life around John McDonnell's ill-fated campaigns to muster enough other MPs' signatures to stand for Labour leadership. The loosely associated magazine *Red Pepper* cavils from the wings, based on a peculiarly northern English intellectual and political sensibility valiantly trying to maintain a 'rainbow coalition' of old Labour and newer 'social forces'. The purpose of this essay is to see what else if anything is left of the Labour left, especially its more mainstream elements, and if it does still exist, where it draws its inspiration from. The task is especially urgent now Labour looks set for a prolonged period in parliamentary opposition, when it tends to rediscover its ostensibly leftist 'conscience' in the mists of moral maximalism, windy rhetoric and workerist sentimentality.

## *Compass: "Ghostbusters of the Left"*

Within a generally bleak British political landscape, especially in and around the Labour Party, the 'left wing pressure group' Compass offers some sign of intelligent life. Its most prominent MP Jon Cruddas is about the only one of Labour's leaders who hasn't been fatally tainted by the New Labour years, and looks fair set to inherit the mantle of Labour's 'conscience-keeper' in its coming wilderness period, especially now he has proved his political mettle by beating off the local challenge of the BNP (alongside neighbouring MP and rather unlikely anti-fascist Margaret Hodge). Its personable chairperson Neal Lawson is a thoughtful, constructive contributor to radio and TV debate about what goes on around Westminster, a dogged motivator and skilful organiser. Compass associates can be relied upon to talk relative sense, and its publications are well written and researched, and (unusually on the left) very well designed and presented. Its events are for the most part well run, stimulating and collaborative, within a recognisably 'Labour fringe' model of top-table speakers and appreciative if occasionally disgruntled audience. Unusually in mainstream politics, it has attracted large numbers of young people, just about – or so it seems – everyone under the age of thirty actively involved in Labour politics, and not surprisingly has recently 'taken over' Labour Youth.

The Compass website is a model of its kind: attractive, easy to navigate and updated on a daily or even hourly basis. Compass campaigns are highly professional and competent, with eye-catching themes and slogans, a focus on what can realistically be achieved and a genuinely broad range of support, aiming (if not always managing) to reach beyond the established parliamentary and party political networks. It has recruited over 4000 members and three full-time staff in five years of existence, and claims over 25,000 email contacts (compared to a reported less than 50,000 for the whole Labour Party, which says a lot about the larger and subsidiary organisations' relative states of health).[21] Its participatory membership may be closer to the 600 who took part in an important vote on support for tactical voting just before the election. But then all political groups have different levels of membership involvement. Of all the individuals and groups jostling for advantage in

---

[21] Neal Lawson and Gavin Hayes' speeches to Compass AGM 14th November 2009

and around the 'post-New' or (the older Miliband's absurd formulation) "next" Labour Party, Compass seems better placed than most to achieve its stated aim of providing "direction for the democratic left."

So what's wrong with Compass? My argument put simply is that, with all its talk of 'renewal' and 'modernisation', apparently busy and purposeful 'campaigning' on the issues of the day, and assiduous use of new technologies and political techniques, Compass is a pale $21^{st}$ century retread of older political forms; specifically the factional tradition of the Labour left most recently represented by the Labour Co-ordinating Committee (LCC) (1978-98), where many older Compass leaders and activists cut their political teeth. Then at an even ghostlier remove – across the apparently decisive but always blurred and permeable dividing line between British 'reformism' and 'revolution' – Compass/LCC owes a major historical debt to the more democratic, 'modern', open and popular elements of the Communist Party of Great Britain (CPGB) (1920-91).[22] To take a most recent example: Compass' promotion of 'tactical voting' at the 2010 general election, described by Neal Lawson as "groundbreaking" and seriously "risky" in Labour Party terms because it appears to endorse other parties' candidates, takes up the theme of a decade earlier from 'Make Votes Count' and the

---

[22] I have examined elsewhere the influence of the CPGB, specifically its 'Euro-communist' wing and the magazine *Marxism Today*, on the modern Labour Party and the formation of its New Labour elite; A. Pearmain, *Antonio Gramsci and the Politics of New Labour* (London 2010).

'New Politics Network', the slightly shadowy successors to the Democratic Left, which is what the CPGB became on dissolution.

I am aware of the knock-on political perils of this argument. One of the abiding features of the Labour right has been its anti-communism, and in the labyrinthine and frequently internecine strife that has constituted Labour politics, the right has never hesitated to accuse the left of facilitating or even representing 'communist infiltration'. If Compass is, as I shall argue, the contemporary umbrella for much of what remains of the Labour left (or as Neal Lawson puts it slightly wearily, its "Ghostbusters; who ya gonna call?"), its opponents on the Labour right may yet in their own post-New Labour desperation deploy those ancient prejudices; another kind of ghostbusting perhaps. Other than forbidding such an abuse in the name of historical truth, and pointing out that the Labour right has plenty of embarrassing historical associations of its own (e.g. Stalin's Fabian cheerleaders, or Mussolini and Pinochet's Labourist admirers), there's not a lot I can do about it. It would be strange if any variant of social democracy were not somehow influenced by other elements within the 'broad church' of Marxist-derived socialism. Compass is simply the latest example of Labour borrowing without attribution from a more rigorous but deeply stigmatised body of thought.

In just the same way that the doomed, conflicted CPGB, with its opposing and self-neutralising strategies of "militant labourism" and "revolutionary democracy", ultimately served little more historical function than generating new ideas,

personnel and energies for the Labour Party – a
"ginger group" was the term used by its own
internal critics – so does Compass sit on the edge
of Labour, one foot in and one foot out, *"with the
perspective of transforming the Labour Party by
remote control"* (as 'Euro-communist' dissident
Pat Devine said of the 1977 *British Road to
Socialism*, the CPGB programme) but actually
exercising precious little real control or even
influence on Labour's mysterious inner workings.[23]
Rather, Compass – effectively positioned and
historically identified in function, politics and
personnel (I would argue) as the 'New Labour left'
– is enabling the Labour Party to live beyond its
'natural' span, long after the founding ideology of
Labourism, its social base among the labouring
masses and its power base in the trade unions have
been dispersed. At least the CPGB had the integrity
to disband – however questionably, given that its
replacements proved unsustainable – when a
majority of those few left felt it had outlived its
usefulness. In keeping Labour alive, Compass is
consuming political energies that would be better
spent elsewhere.

Instead of providing precious artificial life support
to Labourism, Compass could be helping to create
some new political form (and, at its margins and
almost in spite of itself, already is) for a more
promising, truly modern, broadly based and
intelligent left-wing politics in Britain, most likely
configured around the political 'ecologism' of the
Green Party and the emergent-hegemonic
'common sense' of practical, popular

---

[23] G. Andrews, *Endgames and New Times* (London 2004) pp.
163/166, and *Opening the Books* (London 1995), pp. 239/241

environmentalism. Compass is trying hard to align itself with this most promising of the 'new social movements', but ultimately everything depends on whether Compass is in or out of the Labour Party. On the horns of this age-old left wing dilemma it remains impaled yet stubbornly non-committal (Neal Lawson at least acknowledges that there is *"real tension"* between these alternative directions).[24] Is Compass a life-raft out of the wreckage for the Labour Party's more principled and committed and more expansively 'left wing' activists? Or is it a life-belt for the whole sorry crew to hang on to while they seek a more congenial, 'renewed' and 'modern' vessel for an essentially unchanged centrist politics of electoral fix and parliamentary machination? It could – as Compass advocates will say when pushed (drawing explicitly on the key Euro-communist concept of 'contingency', itself derived from the Gramscian understanding of political agency and responsibility) – go either way.

Of course Labour may just make the decision for everybody, by imploding and disbanding itself, and casting all its dwindling band of passengers adrift. This is one of the prospects canvassed by the 'progressive commentariat', alongside proportional representation at Westminster (recently described by Jon Cruddas as *"the route to a new political terrain"*) and the much longed-for 'realignment' of British politics.[25] I would be surprised; the Labour Party is "a remarkably resilient beast", as a local council leader once put it to me. Its collective

---

[24] N. Lawson, speech to Compass AGM 2009
[25] J. Cruddas MP, speech to Compass AGM, 14th November 2009

mood remains surprisingly upbeat, at least in public, consoled even in defeat by the avoidance of 'meltdown'. As the 2010 election demonstrated, the 'meltdown' of any historic party is a very slow process in Britain's sclerotic electoral system, even under the promised 'alternative vote' (which simply gives you more of what you've already got). Labour can still summon the genie of subaltern anti-Conservatism in the north British 'heartlands' where its MPs are now clustered. Labour 'events' – conferences and fringe meetings and 'rallies' – do not 'feel' like those of a disintegrating party, and it takes a conscious effort of will to remember the statistics of plummeting membership, income and activity which indicate that it is.

There has always been a gulf between the 'feel' and the reality of the Labour Party, which is one of the things that keeps it going. This is the anthropological function for the Labour 'tribe' of the repeated expressions of hope for the future and glorification of the past you hear at any party gathering (including Compass events), to guide it through a murky and unpromising present. The Labour Party has survived worse crises than its current one, and there are too many people with vested interests in its survival, not least its indirect but notable beneficiaries amongst the British ruling class. One of Margaret Thatcher's most astute but least noticed epigrams was that *"the Labour Party will never die"*, uttered in 1983 at the height of the Social Democratic Party (SDP) apostasy, the year of Labour's worst post-war general election result (just one percentage point worse than 2010). The 'Labour question' is about more than the party's survival: rather, whether it makes a suitable vehicle (and ever really has) for a left-wing politics with serious transformative intent and effect.

## *Labour's Absorptions*

Labour tradition (which it has far more of than 'history') abounds in examples of vigorous social movements, usually but not always on the left, being courted at a safe distance from the party's main (especially electoral) activities and purposes. We might view Compass' relative openness – what Neal Lawson calls "reaching out to other progressives", exemplified by the controversial invitation to Green MEP Caroline Lucas to address the June 2009 Compass rally – and its astute use of up-to-the-minute styling and technologies as a contemporary example.[26] In its willingness to draw on non-traditional oppositional sources like environmentalism, anti-poverty campaigns and other voluntary organisations and 'NGOs', Compass is Labour's modern point of contact with the new-style "Internet-age campaigning and social networking".[27]

It is no coincidence that these overtures are being made in the context of Labour losing the 2010 general election. Especially in the expectation or aftermath of political defeat, Labour has habitually created selective openings to the non-party left and its self-styled intellectuals; Caroline Lucas is trailed as a principal speaker at the post-defeat 2010 Compass rally, a positive attraction rather

---

[26] Lawson told the 2009 Compass AGM, when asked by people from Brighton (Lucas' constituency) how people should vote in the forthcoming general election, that "the game is to keep the Tories out – think for yourselves".
[27] N. Lawson, G. Hayes, speeches to Compass AGM 2009

than coded provocation to Labour traditionalists. These openings are usually accompanied by siren cries of 'Yes, what you've got to say is really interesting' and 'But what else is there except Labour?' They invariably turn out to lead into dead ends of demoralisation and disappointment, but they always look 'interesting' to begin with. New Labour – which, lest we forget, received a relatively sympathetic hearing all across the left in its early days – is only the most recent and rawest example.

There is usually a time-lag of some years between the formation of these new ideas and their absorption into the Labour bloodstream – and initially at least a vigorous 'immune response' against them – but sooner or later 'this great movement of ours' opens up and admits limited ideological infection in safely neutralised form, suitably adapted to the Labour tradition. Think of it, to extend the immunological metaphor to breaking point, as a kind of political vaccination. Objectively (to use an old-fashioned analytical term) and historically (in this milieu, another), Compass represents just such an opening to Labour's left flank. It purports to provide 'direction for the democratic left' (and that – the name of the short-lived, thoroughgoing 'Euro-communist' successor (1991-2000) to the CPGB – should give us another clue to what Compass is a Labourist opening to), without ever saying or seeming to really understand what that political category might mean or who it might involve.

There have been many other such examples of Labour's selective absorptions from the left – from the parliamentary ultra-leftism of Bennery to the

Hobsbawm-flavoured 'favourite Marxism' of Neil Kinnock and the 'new times' of New Labour. Oddly enough, many of the central personnel of Compass have undergone similarly exploitative treatment (firmly inside the Labour 'tent') at the clammy hands of New Labour, which explains some of these ex-advisers', ex-researchers' and in some cases ex-ministers' current ire towards 'the project'. Within their talk of further 'renewal', and of New Labour being neither 'new' nor 'Labour' enough, there is anger and resentment that they too have been taken for a ride on the Blair/Brown bandwagon (and in some cases jettisoned from it).

There is also an issue about the way the Labour Party 'does politics', and what holds its networks of fractious allegiance and mutual obligation together. A whole chain of flattery, seduction and abuse is going on here, far beneath the media furore about honours and expenses, which taps into the underlying personal motivations – to "serve the people", to "make a difference", to be heard and acclaimed – for often limited people in the process of constructing party and parliamentary political careers. This personal-political corruption runs right across the 'democratic' or 'centre-left', inside Labour and beyond, among a substantial chunk of the currently reviled 'political class', and becomes all too evident when you yourself have been cast aside (usually the occasion for conversion to forms of 'new politics' like electoral reform or 'progressive alliance'). This is a profoundly dishonest and manipulative politics, destructive of people and principle, deeply rooted in British public life and instantly recognisable to those of us with memories that go back beyond the bright new today. Compass is in part where old New Labourists go to die.

Or is this an uncharitable and narrow-minded interpretation? Unnecessarily and destructively purist? Or even, as the Compass-aligned editor of *Soundings* magazine described a previous version of this commissioned essay when I submitted it, some new form of that other time-honoured British left wing tradition: 'blinkered and self-defeating sectarianism'?[28] Could the Labour appropriation of Euro-communist ideas be an example of healthy cross-fertilisation, as the more thoughtful and historically aware Compass-ites argue? Well, the proof of the historical pudding and all that; even the most generous assessment of the present state of health of the 'democratic left' in Britain has to be that (beyond Compass, and dwindling assets of the CP legacy like the magazine *Soundings*) it barely exists.[29] There is what we might call a large and diffuse 'cultural left', a loose network of affiliations, 'communities of interest or affect', like-minded individuals and friendship circles – some of them taking on firm organisational or sub-cultural form (readership of *The Guardian* the most obvious) – but it no longer constitutes any kind of organised force able to exercise concerted pressure towards any specific common aim, let alone its historical objective of 'socialism'.

---

[28] Curiously, Compass chairperson Neal Lawson was much more receptive, and has even used some of my themes in recent speeches! Labourism remains receptive and adaptable...

[29] Another of those ex-CP assets, the 'militant labourist' newspaper *The Morning Star,* was the only publication on sale outside the 2009 Compass AGM, much to participants' wry amusement.

As such, the 'democratic left' stands at the end-point of a process of defeat and disorientation which began in the 1970s and reached its climax in the extraordinary 'new times' of the late 1980s and early '90s. With 'the collapse of communism' and the deepening hegemony of neoliberal capitalism, not to mention the wilfully confusing cultural ideology of postmodernism and the accompanying politics of artifice and 'positioning', the left (to quote the venerable 'First New Left'-ies Mike Rustin and Stuart Hall) made *"unfortunate concessions to values that are probably better simply regarded as those of the other side"*, and in particular facilitated the New Labour accommodation of Thatcherism by *"hero-ising consumption"*.[30] We have yet to reckon with, or even recognise, the full effects and implications of that dismal experience. But then the British 'democratic left', especially its Labour and Communist components in their traditional demeanour of headlong rush towards a more 'hopeful' future, has a long history of falsifying, forgetting or on occasions deliberately obliterating its own history.

## *Where does Compass come from?*

To judge from the Compass website and associated publications, you would never guess that the organisation has any origins of its own; it's as though it sprang out of nowhere the day before yesterday, with a bunch of ready formed signature 'issues' and supporters and political styles (the great socialist historian Raphael Samuel observed

---

[30] M. Rustin, in S. Hall & M. Jacques, *New Times* (London 1989), p. 314; S. Hall, personal interview 6th January 2004

the same amnesia in the latter-day *Marxism Today*, which he found *"singularly bereft of historical articles"*[31]). The Labour Party often exhibits a curious historical amnesia all its own (again, a prop for its determined optimism), most obviously and recently in the wilful 'newness' of New Labour, but its various wings are inclined to craft their own particular competing and usually self-serving mythologies. A couple were aired at the 2009 Compass AGM. Firstly, Jon Cruddas mourned the abandonment of *"the historical Labour mission to change the world... its defining lodestar"*, even though the Party's stated ambitions have always been limited to the nation-state and the more or less immediately practicable. Labour may have vaguely wished to change the country, but changing the world has been left to Ernest Bevin's *"idle dreamers"*. Secondly, Compass vice-chair Sue Goss, in appealing to the municipal localism and cultural alternativism which underwrote various forms of 1970s-era 'community action', bemoaned the fact that *"Labour has forgotten how to act in civil society"*, ignoring the fact that it has always focused its attentions on the 'political society' of parliament, councils and the state.

In recent times Compass has been preoccupied with exposing and resisting the most blatantly Thatcherite inheritance of the fading New Labour project (which, to support my 'delayed infection' theory, *Marxism Today* did in 1998 with its special 'Wrong!' issue); especially anything to do with 'Lord of Darkness' Peter Mandelson, who is so profoundly loathed within the 'labour movement'

---

[31] R. Samuel, *The Lost World of British Communism* (London 2006), pp. 29/30

you have to wonder why it's treated him so well[32]. Not surprisingly, this tone of disaffection has enabled Compass to become a repository for anything and anyone who feels at all jarred-off with the state of the contemporary Labour Party, from old fashioned and largely unreconstructed Bennites to the most recently jettisoned New Labour fellow traveller. If you look closely at who actually takes part in Compass conferences and on-line debates, you'll find a common bond of loyally oppositional discontent.

While other more traditional left wing vehicles like Tribune or the Campaign for Labour Party Democracy fade away, the far more *a la mode* Compass seems to have drawn into itself pretty much everyone to the left of Tony Blair, i.e. pretty much everyone. Neal Lawson is rightly proud of having *"given a lot of people something to hope for"*.[33] Its freshness and novelty have given the Labour malcontents a new lease of life, or at least some sense that there may still be some life left in the party of which most have been lifelong members. Again, Euro-communism provides a historical and temperamental model, as a last rallying cry for exhausted, departing CP dissidents (who also, as it turned out, had temporarily submerged their own multiple micro-differences in the cause of expedient anti-Stalinist macro-unity). Neal Lawson at least acknowledges this source when pressed: *"Compass derives a huge amount of inspiration from that kind of politics."*

---

[32] The answer's obvious; he – usually – wins elections
[33] Neal Lawson, personal interview 27th May 2009; unless otherwise indicated, all Neal Lawson quotes come from this interview

But if, at least in conversation with me, he recognises a debt to Euro-communism, the rest of Compass locates itself firmly within Labourism. For all its shiny initiatives and up-to-the-moment brand-identity, a very particular tradition within a tradition is just about discernible: the shifting crowd of fixers and visionaries usually referred to as the 'Labour left'. The current mood of Compass – stoic resignation at the apparent hopelessness of the Labour cause, head-shaking bemusement at the last actions of New Labour in government, talk of the Party itself being "necessary but not sufficient" and more than a hint that it's time to make for the life rafts – itself has a long history, right back to 'Tory Marxist' and 'social imperialist' H.M. Hyndman's despairing 1920 observation *"No hope but in the Labour Party, and not much in that."*[34] Bevan and Cripps and the other 'Popular Front' Labourists of the 1930s displayed the same ambivalence and disenchantment towards the temporarily subdued mother party in its post-MacDonald narrowness and self-absorption, and were briefly expelled for it. Various schools of post-war Labour intellectuals would make veiled or not so veiled threats to give up on the party unless it paid them more respect; until the SDP did just that, and foundered on their own vanities and the institutional inertia of the parliamentary political system.[35]

---

[34] C. Tsuzuki, *H.M. Hyndman* (London 1961)

[35] R. Desai, *Intellectuals and Socialism* (London 1995); I. Crewe & A. King, *SDP* (London 1995). The SDP, as Crewe and King put it, *"went up like a rocket and came down like the stick."*

Popular affection for and attachment to Labour has always been shallow; the party has rarely commanded a substantial majority of even working class support, and for only a tiny minority has it gone beyond electoral routine; the political equivalent of going to church at Christmas into anything resembling political activism. Repeated attempts to create a genuinely 'mass party' have always failed (with the arguable exception of the immediate post-Second World War period, which was historically exceptional for the whole British left). Strangely, the CP – perhaps too readily taking the Labour left at its own estimation – always described the Labour Party as "the mass party of the working class", when Labour's active membership was rarely much higher than its own, especially outside election periods. But then another oddity (and failure) of the CPGB was that its relationship with its own country was almost always mediated by the Labour Party.

Labour's 'social atmosphere' is frequently rancorous, and occasionally poisonous. People in the Labour Party don't seem to enjoy the experience much, to like their comrades, or to 'belong' to the organisation in the way Communists (with what Samuel called their "complete social identity"), Conservatives or even Liberals did and do.[36] Compass has that same heavily conditional attachment to the Labour Party, counterbalanced by an equally historical terror of 'the political wilderness' outside (curious term that, when Labour's inner life is an all too real political wilderness), and underwritten by the traditional

[36] R. Samuel, *The Lost World of British Communism* (London 2007)

75

Labourist devices of loyalty, "will to unity" and sacrifice, and the primary tribal glue of visceral, subaltern and generally unreasoned anti-Conservatism.

## *The Unwritten Rules of Labour Factionalism*

As well as heir to an intellectual tradition within a generally anti-intellectual tradition, Compass is also a functioning Labour faction. The British left is notoriously forgetful – one of the reasons it keeps making the same mistakes – but there is in this country a long and (it has to be said) fascinating history of sectarian and factional activity, more or less constructive or subversive, more or less open or dishonest, more or less collaborative or nasty. It may be inherent in the nature of political action, but compared to radical or 'progressive' political movements in other countries, the British left is unusually "fissiparous" (a term much used by Raphael Samuel). There is nothing we seem to enjoy more than a good fight amongst ourselves. We have generally conducted our political relations on the principle articulated by Amadeo Bordiga, Gramsci's early colleague and rival in the Italian Communist Party (and target of Lenin's ire in *Left Wing Communism – An Infantile Disorder)* that *"Nothing clears the air like a good split."*[37] More recently and closer to home, *Life of Brian* got it pretty much spot on. This of course is the prime reason the left in Britain has been weaker and less effective than pretty much

---

[37] G. A. Williams, *Proletarian Order* (London 1975); the Italian left has also been historically 'fissiparous' and profligate with political opportunity.

anywhere else in the world, despite frequently favourable historical circumstances; if you can't agree amongst yourselves, you've not got much chance of getting anyone else on your side. And if you keep on disagreeing amongst yourselves over matters of petty detail, you will continue to squander whatever political opportunities and 'contingencies' present themselves.

The Labour Party, for all its periodic purges of groups and individuals, and generally assiduous patrolling of its left flank for signs of organised infiltration (especially from the direction of the Communist Party, whose formal overtures were persistently rebuffed, and more recently 'entryist' Trotskyists), has always had competing factions trying to take it in one direction or another. They're not called factions, which are prohibited under the terms of the party constitution; they must also take great care not to look like a separate 'party within a party' like Militant or less blatantly Socialist Organiser in the 1980s, or to involve members of other parties which stand candidates against Labour's (the cause of recent minor controversy over 'Green-wooing' within Compass). To avoid proscription, they usually sail under some flag of convenience like a newspaper, parliamentary interest-group, lobby or think tank, but in their internal workings and external relations they have all the functional attributes of organised factions, promoting a certain viewpoint, interest or set of policies. The 'broad church' party has managed, with occasional convulsions and expulsions, to hold it all in check with certain loosely defined but highly effective rules (in the nature of Henry Drucker's Labour "ethos", a quasi-anthropological concept he applies with enormous insight to the Labour 'tribe').[38]

Firstly, you have to respect the party's main *raison d'être*, which is to get MPs elected (and individually re-elected) to parliament. A commitment to parliamentarism is essential, even if it co-exists with notional 'extra-parliamentary struggle' and harks back to a historically hazy tradition of popular democracy where MPs bestride the dazzled nation as 'tribunes of the people'. This is above all what secures Labour to the status quo. Secondly, less important now but historically central, you have to defer to the party's principal backers in the trade unions. The 'brothers' supplied the dosh (and still do, an amazing 73 per cent of party income in 2006). In the old days "the dead souls of Labourism" (Tom Nairn's phrase for the much-derided union block vote) swung decisively behind 'sensible' policies and leaders, usually on the anti-communist right. It was the breakdown of this 'top table' Labour settlement which caused the last major inner-party convulsion in the 1970s and '80s.

For all the talk of democracy and accountability, firstly in the left's reselection of MPs and leadership electoral college, then the right's One Member One Vote, the most significant change in Labour politics over that period was the diminution of the unions' institutional power. This was how the modern Labour Party sought to resolve the historic conflict between class and national interests which had always undermined its political

---

[38] H. Drucker, *Doctrine and Ethos in the Labour Party* (Edinburgh 1979)

impact, especially in government. These days the trade unions peddle a much more amorphous 'influence', in keeping with their vastly reduced status in broader society and economy. This means there are benefits to the parliamentary party leadership in confronting the unions occasionally and on very carefully chosen grounds, where the union case is essentially sectionalist and anti-business, and their public support weak. Otherwise, the brothers are kept on board with regular contact and patronage, not least because even the most disenchanted can still be called upon to support favourable party or factional activity (as with the Communication Workers Union's funding of Compass' campaign against Royal Mail part-privatisation).

Thirdly, you avoid going into honest detail on any grand transformative project you wish to bring to the public affairs of the party and the country. If you mention 'socialism', you have to make clear that it is something that happened in the past or might yet happen in the distant future, one of the party's 'values' that you acknowledge and honour. But you carefully avoid practical detail on how it might apply to the present. You only admit, to yourselves or anyone else, certain campaign themes, immediate objectives and above all (the main currency of Labour debate) 'policy proposals', things the government should adopt and at least pledge to implement to alleviate some specific social problem or state inefficiency. Anything more ambitious, transformative or truly 'revolutionary', is liable to get you booted out or (perhaps worse) roundly ignored. This is all as true of the Labour left as of the right; the only practical difference is in how loudly they proclaim their 'socialism', the volume of their 'maximalism'.

Fourthly, you restrict your activity and membership to the party itself; you can talk to people outside, but you do not involve them in your tactical or strategic decisions, and you steer well clear of any serious challenge (electoral or otherwise) they might pose to Labour. Ultimately, through your trials and triumphs, joys and tribulations, functions and dysfunctions, you keep it all in the Labour 'family'. Your political and organisational focus is on 'winning positions' in the party for your people and your policies; so that much of the party's inner life represents a kind of political 'sibling rivalry', jostling for attention (both positive and negative) from the wider clan. The strange spectacle of the Miliband brothers competing for the party leadership (with much excited speculation over which one Compass backs) is only the most graphic recent example.

Compass abides by all these largely unwritten rules. On this four-point 'test' it fits comfortably into the long and not always honourable tradition of Labour factionalism. For example, its chairperson cites as one of its main achievements the fact that "*One of our people recently became the chair of Young Labour. That's quite something, to beat the machine and take a position.*" He also insists that Compass is not a faction, on the basis that it looks out beyond the Labour Party "*and wants to form relationships with people outside*", but so far they have not taken concrete form. We might also consider the group's relative extroversion and receptiveness to non-Labour people and ideas a symptom of the bigger party's desperation and dereliction. There's not a lot happening in the Labour Party (including, if reports are to be believed, in recently Compass-ed Young Labour) so Compass has to go looking for new friends elsewhere, another historical function of Labour factions during hard times. It also makes sure to keep in touch with its friends in high places: it supported Gordon Brown's unopposed 2008 leadership campaign – for no obvious reason, and to the considerable annoyance of large sections of its own members and supporters – and its other prominent MP Jon Trickett discreetly moved across soon after to become Brown's Parliamentary Private Secretary.[39] Jon Cruddas is constantly courted as the lesser stub of some 'dream ticket' or other; his demure rebuffs are never especially strenuous.

## *The Labour Coordinating Committee*

Compass' more recent and specific origins are to be found in the Labour left of the 1970s and '80s, in particular the factional organisation and publications of the Labour Coordinating Committee which emerged from the wreckage of the Bennite hard left. The LCC was established in 1978, as a 'policy' counterpart to the 'constitutional' pressure group the Campaign for Labour Party Democracy, with a more consciously public profile and political role than the CLPD.

---

[39] Shortly before becoming Brown's PPS, Trickett had told me that in his view the Labour Party was finished, and that Compass was indeed partly designed as a 'life raft' (the first such usage of the term I'd heard) for the 'democratic left'; J. Trickett MP, personal conversation. For Compass' most recent turn against Brown (for, as Neal Lawson puts it, "flunking it"), see *The Guardian,* 18th November 2009.

Both were based on profound disillusionment with the 1970s 'old Labour' governments of Wilson and Callaghan, a formative experience for all elements of the 'movement' but felt especially acutely among the new influx of educated, public sector professionals drawn to Labour in the aftermath of 1968. Their common aim was to prevent any future Labour government from "reneging on its manifesto commitments", while avoiding the more traditional Labour factional activities of "fund raising and MP fan clubs". Instead, the LCC set itself the founding task (according to its first Secretary Nigel Stanley) of *"actually winning support for socialist ideas"* and the creation of *"a mass party"*, primarily through Labour conference fringe meetings, and conferences and pamphlets of its own. While its focus remained firmly on the inner life of the party, it also sought positions of leadership and policy in the trade unions, and collaboration with the influential trade union 'Broad Lefts'.[40] As such, the LCC began life as what McSmith calls *"a Bennite ginger group"*.[41]

The most striking feature of those early LCC pamphlets, examined retrospectively, is the way they take ideas and insights from the 'broader left', specifically the 'Euro-communist' and *Marxism Today* wing of the CPGB, and some years after their inception attempt to apply them to internal Labour Party debate.[42] So *Labour and Mass*

---

[40] D. & M. Kogan, *The Battle for the Labour Party* (London 1982), pp. 50/53

[41] A. McSmith, *Faces of Labour* (London 1998), p. 63

[42] The 'Euros' and *Marxism Today* were actually quite distinct from the 'militant labourists' of the CP's industrial wing in the TU 'Broad Lefts', who were clustered around the ex-CP newspaper *Morning Star;* this created further, largely

*Politics – Rethinking our Strategy,* written by
Charles Clarke and David Griffiths and published
in 1982, draws inspiration from Eric Hobsbawm's
seminal 1978 **Marxism Today** article *"The
Forward March of Labour Halted?"* in its scathing
observation of *"the Labour Party's narrowing
electoral base, tenuous links with other progressive
forces, over-identification with bureaucratic state
structures and uninspiring inner-party routines."* A
whole section devoted to *"Learning from other
movements"* pursues the 'new social forces' from
the CP's 1977 revision of *The British Road to
Socialism,* with its familiar checklist of *"women,
ethnic minorities and youth organisations"* (we'll
pay another visit to the 1977 *BRS* later).

But there is neither open acknowledgment of these
external sources nor genuine engagement with the
aims and concerns of the 'new social forces': *"the
relationship of the party to these potential allies
can only be worked out in practice, and we lay
down no blueprints"* (this refusal to specify, often
justified as a commitment to 'contingency' and
open-mindedness, and touted as one of the 'lessons
of feminism', was also characteristic of latter day
'Euro-communism'). And again the practical focus
is on Labour's internal politics: *"Whilst our
support has been growing among activists the left's
base is weak amongst ordinary rank and file
supporters and union members... we need to
concentrate on building our extra-parliamentary
base."*[43] How well connected the CP was to the

destructive cultural and political crosscurrents within the '80s
CP/LP 'democratic left'.
[43] C. Clarke & D. Griffiths, *Labour And Mass Politics –
Rethinking our Strategy* (LCC 1982); this and other cited

'new social forces' is a moot point; the 'Euro-communists' frequently complained that the party's commitment to the 'broad democratic alliance' was rhetorical and *post-hoc*, always itself a few years behind the new 'identity politics', which meant that by the time 'new ideas' reached Labour they were even older.[44]

*Reconstruction - How the Labour Party – and the Left – can win*, written by John Denham and published in 1984, is an attempt to come to terms with "the disaster of June 9th" 1983, Labour's 'suicide note' general election. Again, there is implicit reference to (apocryphally, new Labour leader Neil Kinnock's 'favourite Marxist') Hobsbawm's obituary for classical Labourism, in the observation that "*The social and economic conditions which enabled right wing social democracy to achieve some success have passed.*" But there is now also recognition of Stuart Hall's accompanying argument about the emergence of hegemonic Thatcherism, as the new "common sense" of the epoch, first elaborated in his 1979 *Marxism Today* article "The Great Moving Right Show" and immediately taken up by other Gramscians (and fiercely resisted by the 'militant labourists'). Our 'time-lag' between Euro-communist inception and Labour absorption is now

---

LCC pamphlets are stored in the Labour Party archive at the People's History Museum, Manchester.
[44] S. Rowbotham, *Beyond the Fragments* (London 1980) includes several appreciative references to 'Euro-communism', while mounting a fierce critique of the traditional Leninist party form the broader CP nearly always stuck to until it ceased to matter.

five years.[45] Shortly afterwards (as if to illustrate that the process could work the other way), the term 'Democratic Left' appeared in the title of another LCC pamphlet, some five years *before* it was adopted by the successor organisation to the disbanded CPGB![46] It was also adopted as a factional name by LCC supporters in the National Union of Students, who had 'taken over' NUS in 1982 (not a pretty sight; I was there).

*New Maps for the Nineties – A Third Road Socialist Reader*, published in 1990, represents an early public appearance by future Compass chairperson but then trade union official Neal Lawson, who edited this collection of essays on the general theme of "The Crisis of the British Left" (and showed some of the design flair which would later characterise Compass). In keeping with the common upsurge in left wing 'optimism of the intellect' of the late 1980s and a determination after a decade of 'high Thatcherism' to look on the bright side of 'new times' – what Slavoj Zizek sardonically calls *"the beginning of the 'happy 1990s'... the advent of a global, liberal world community lurking just around the corner"* – the pamphlet is a positive attempt to flesh out a "Third Road – a politics which explicitly seeks to break with the two dominant traditions of 20th century European Socialism – gradualist reformism and Leninist insurrectionism".[47] This includes a sympathetic section by veteran Labour leftist

---

[45] J. Denham, *Reconstruction - How the Labour Party – and the left – can win* (LCC 1984)
[46] LCC (no named author), *A Strategy for the Democratic Left* (undated, but most likely mid-1980s)
[47] S. Zizek, "Post-Wall", *London Review of Books* 19th November 2009

Trevor Fisher on Gramsci, his conception of *"socialism as a process of change"* and the *"importance of pre-figurative activity"*, some fifteen-odd years now after the onset of the original Euro-communist application of British 'Gramscism'.

There is also by now a strong sense of disillusionment in the leadership of Neil Kinnock, who shows *"little intellectual or theoretical substance behind the socialist rhetoric"*. This 'third road' would most definitely not lead towards 'The Third Way'; or would it? Neal Lawson now puts it like this: *"the way the LCC developed politically from '81 is the story of the Kinnock years, the way projects start from principles in a left wing direction, then after successive election defeats they become more about chasing power."* This marks the estrangement, exacerbated by the late-1980s Labour Party Policy Review, between the 'soft left' (with the LCC at its core) and the Kinnockite officials, advisers and politicians (marshalled by former LCC pamphleteer and critic of *"bureaucratic state structures"*, Charles Clarke) who were busily centralising control of the party in the parliamentary leader's office. The historically transitional character of Kinnock's leadership, the 'deck-clearing' precondition for New Labour, comes through in *New Maps for the Nineties'* plaintive *"in the absence of strong democratic socialist forces, accommodation to the centre becomes almost inevitable."*[48]

---

[48] N. Lawson (ed.), *New Maps for the Nineties – A Third Road Socialist Reader* (LCC 1990)

By 1993, just such an accommodation is evident in the LCC's *Modernising Britain*, alongside the absorption of the 'New Times' analysis of the state of modern Britain advanced by *Marxism Today* in 1987/9 (back to a five year gap!), which is semi-reverentially caricatured as *"an army of academics proclaiming the coming of the information society and a post-industrial, post-Fordist future."* There is an explicit link to the 'personalisation' strand within 'New Times' (initiated by Charlie Leadbeater's 1987 *MT* article "Power to the Person", and recently a central theme in New Labour's 'public sector reforms') in *Modernising Britain's* advocacy of *"choice and customisation... People must feel that they are individuals with their own rights and autonomy in their dealings with the welfare state"*. But again, after further superficial analysis of *"hopelessly old"* Britain, the pamphlet falls back on the more comfortable terrain of what Labour should do to itself. To the historic problem of a *"state that has been unable to develop the right kind of relationship with wealth creation"* the answer is that "Labour must modernise itself." The final four pages (in a pamphlet of fifteen) concerns itself with "Modernising Labour", through constitutional reforms like OMOV (One Member One Vote) in every party election and (a sign of the dwindling power of the labour movement's 'industrial wing') the abolition of the trade union block vote.

The internal political significance of these procedural changes for the Labour left was in marking a final clear divide (already signalled in Pat Seyd's seminal mid-1980s *New Socialist* article "Bennism without Benn") between LCC and its erstwhile constitutional counterparts in the CLPD on the terrain of 'modernisation'. But within all this there are signs of other new strains within the Labour family: *"It sometimes seems as if the only role the membership has in today's Party is in providing a database of names and addresses for fund raising appeals and a source of workers at election times."* This is described as *"the massive but passive approach to membership"*, with the leadership given a free hand in the party's public presentation: *"Party members are not even surprised any more when they read in* **The Guardian** *that Labour now believes in an entirely new economics, when they know that at best no more than twenty people would have seen the draft before it is leaked to the press... the days of mass membership political organisations are over, particularly as the Party has no clear idea what its membership is there for."*[49]

By this stage you get the distinct impression that the LCC has run out of steam, partly because the baton of 'modernisation' has been firmly grasped by New Labour: as Neal Lawson describes it, *"Blair comes in, everything's transformed but by then he has control of the machine and he's racing way ahead of the LCC, ditching Clause 4 etc. The organisation had nothing to do because he was doing much more of it, much faster and more powerfully."* Within the party, serious political differences were now emerging that had been masked through the 1980s, *"but at the time those differences weren't allowed the space to appear because you were too busy trying to save the party from utter failure at the polls, infiltration by Militant... There were people that wanted Labour*

---

[49] LCC (no named author), *Modernising Britain* (1993)

*to win again and there were people who wanted to take it over for Trotskyist ends. Within that stark polarisation it was very hard for any kind of nuance to exist."*

## The end of the LCC, Renewal and the emergence of Compass

The Labour Coordinating Committee was wound up in 1998, twenty years and a long way from its "Bennite ginger group" origins. It chose to mark the occasion with publication of its own history, written by Paul Thompson and Ben Lucas, whose second sentence observed with some pride that *"successive generations of LCC are helping run government or the Party machine"*. By now the debt to Hobsbawm is made explicit, in the pamphlet's title *The Forward March of Modernisation* and its recognition of his *"theoretical analysis of why Labour's defeat in 1979 was more than just a blip, but represented a major turning point in which the corporatist Fabian model of post war politics had reached its end. The history of the LCC has been about getting Labour to come to terms with this analysis and to modernise its ideology, politics, style, structure and message."*[50] Of course, by this stage both *Marxism*

---

[50] P. Thompson & B. Lucas, *The Forward March of Modernisation* (LCC 1998); Hobsbawm's article was actually first published in 1978, and offered a much broader critique of all forms of Labourism and its shrivelling base in industrial capitalism, not just of Fabian corporatism. This retrospective 'modernisers' version of "the history of the LCC" is open to question on other counts; for example it wrongly dates the foundation of the 'modernising' journal *Renewal* in 1993, when (according to founder Neal Lawson) it started publication "about '85".

*Today* and the CPGB had disappeared (apart from the one-off 'Wrong!' issue of 1998 and the dwindling band of latter day Euro-communists in the Democratic Left, itself to be wound up soon after), so it was quite safe to lay claim to elements of their legacy.

On that other side of the equation, the 'Euro-communists' had long since realised and understood their position of detached, delayed and selected influence on the process of Labour modernisation; a contemporary application of the traditional 'gadfly' function of communist intellectuals for 'militant labourism' that extends back through the troubled history of relations between the Labour and Communist Parties. As *Marxism Today* editor Martin Jacques told me, *"Labour people would attack us on something – like The Forward March of Labour Halted? – then two years later agree with us"* (as we've seen, the time-lag was usually rather longer). He also recalls a private conversation in 1989 with Peter Mandelson, who said *"We'd never have been able to do it (take over the Labour Party) without you"*; and another in 1991 with Tony Blair, who made plain his utter contempt for Labour and Labourism: *"Other Labour people would only go so far, but he just kept on going..."* [51]

When *Marxism Today* was being wound up in 1991, Jacques could look back with some pride on the magazine's contribution to the debate on how (or whether) the left should respond to Thatcherism, and the 'realignment of the left' it prompted: *"Put crudely, the Bennites, CP*

---

[51] M. Jacques, personal interview, 12th December 2003

*Stalinists, the Trotskyist groups and conservative forces were on one side; and MT, the Euro-communists, the soft left and the Kinnockites were on the other.*"[52] If this was a process of intellectual exploitation, its victims were wholly willing, not to say flattered (as Hobsbawm, launched into a glittering post-communist career as a 'public intellectual' and New Labour associate, quite plainly was). Furthermore, the 1980s/'90s 'realignment of British politics' heralded by 'New Times' was a curiously one-sided affair. The left may have been radically re-orientated but there was no equivalent 'realignment of the right' (that would have to wait a little longer, or had actually already happened). Behind Major's displacement of Thatcher herself, and more recently the Cameroon 'makeover' of the Conservative Party and even coalition with the LibDems, the political and ideological infrastructure of Thatcherism is pretty much intact (not least because New Labour has taken great care not to dismantle it).

For their part, the authors of *The Forward March of Modernisation* (both one-time LCC chairpersons) are also aware of the risks of appropriation by larger political forces, and of the substance within the "*two over-riding myths about LCC: that it was primarily an organisational machine for taking on the hard left; and that it did the ideological dirty work for successive leaderships in swinging the party to the right*" (this latter was of course a major accusatory theme of *MT*'s contemporaneous and embittered "Wrong!"). They also recognise that Labour is most receptive to intellectual provocation in electoral adversity:

---

[52] M. Jacques, *Marxism Today*, December 1991

*"It is an uncomfortable fact that LCC has always been at its best after defeats."* To reconcile the contradictions inherent in these relationships and situations, LCC *"settled into a role of critical support to the new (Kinnock) leadership"*. While they deny close liaison with the 'Kinnockites', *"LCC had to do the slates, the model motions, the identification of speakers"* because *"in those days the Party machine simply did not organise on the conference floor."* Again, for all the talk of 'mass politics', the focus remains on Labour's internal affairs. What really got the LCC going was a good old inner-party wrangle.

When the *"powerful Scottish LCC"* proposed that the national organisation *"accept the 'leading role of the working class', a large number of younger, London-based members primarily out of the student movement arrived by train to sink it."* New polarisations were emerging, between *"a fundamentalist left wedded to a dogmatic version of class politics"* and *"a strategic left, LCC on the inside, Marxism Today and others on the outside, who were developing a pluralistic politics that recognised that Thatcherism was a distinctive enemy and challenge, not just business as usual for capitalism."* So the compliment was retrospectively repaid, in language that echoed *Marxism Today's* own emerging four-cornered analytical model of left/right/radical/ conservative (in case you're wondering, Bennite or 'hard' Labourism was 'left conservative' and Thatcherism was 'right radical') and the shared commitment of "the pragmatic majority" to "political pluralism" (this latter another key code-word of the 'new times').

## *New Labour Emerges*

The same underlying model is evident in the condemnation by Blair and other New Labour figures of "the forces of conservatism" mid-way through his leadership, an outburst that was met (like much of the Third Way) with some bewilderment by the broader political 'commentariat', who were pretty much oblivious to the Euro-communist roots of New Labour. They never really got the underlying nuances of the 'new times' thesis of the late 1980s and early '90s either, with its awed technophilia and its wide-eyed paeans to the liberating 'contingencies' of 'flexible specialisation' and globalisation; and New Labour had no interest in disclosing or acknowledging them. I would argue now that the 'realignment of the left' ushered in by New Times is better described as wholesale disorientation. It's not so much that the 'democratic left' consciously changed its position relative to other forces within the traditional, popularly understood and still prevailing left-right spectrum (the reflex centrist Labour response to defeat), as that it lost (in its customary insularity and self-absorption) any clear sense of its own of where it fitted. Like (by then) its flagship *Marxism Today*, it had (as Martin Jacques puts it) *"floated free"* of its historical moorings.

The process gathered pace after the 'more honourable' 1987 general election defeat when, for all the razzamatazz of Mandelsonian presentation, (for Thompson and Lucas) *"the Party was still addressing a society where millions of union card-carrying men worked in big factories."* LCC played a full part in the subsequent Policy Review, in contrast to the abstemious abstention of the hard left, and in a spirit of *"swallowing our pride and working with those who are interested in winning power."* All the same, it reserved the right to criticize as well as support: the Policy Review was *"saved from mediocrity by the intelligence and creative thinking of key individuals"*, but was otherwise simply a matter of *"dumping unpopular policies"*. Heffernan and Marqusee present a slightly different version in their meticulous but generally poisonous account of the Kinnock years: *"Every year, when its submissions were largely ignored, the LCC would express disappointment with the review's lack of "vision", "strategy", "radicalism" or "priorities", then demand that Party members and conference delegates back it anyway."*[53]

By this time, there is a sense in the LCC's own account of itself that the self-styled *"outriders for change"* are no longer making Labour's political weather – they wanted *"a positive strategy of modernisation (but) Labour never really got to have this fundamental debate"*. These were *"difficult years for avowed modernisers"*, not least because the key figures of New Labour – Blair, Brown, Gould and Mandelson – begin to loom large and to subsume 'debate' within their own electoral and parliamentary ambitions, so that their critical supporters' *"criticism has all but disappeared"*. All they have left to offer a ruthlessly centralised and electorally focused Labour Party is their support. In the process the 'mass politics' of the earlier LCC shrinks to the

---

[53] R. Heffernan & M. Marqusee, *Defeat from the Jaws of Victory* (London 1992), p. 177

'modernisation' of the soft left, which is then absorbed within the 'project' of New Labour. As Lucas and Thompson put it, *"To do anything other than support the leadership in these circumstances would have been the worst kind of self indulgence for the LCC."*

Other kinds of shrinkage are evident within this process: of feminism for example, whose powerful critique of patriarchal social relations and personal identities (of which the Labour Party has been a primary historical site) was reduced to a matter of inner party procedure, in particular quotas and 'women only shortlists' for MP selection; or democracy, which shrank to a proposed Bill of Rights (never enacted) and proportional representation (limited to the electoral margins, and kept well away from Westminster, where it might have made a major difference). There is yet more internal party procedural reform like the 1996 'Commission on Party Democracy', whose stated aim of ensuring that "Labour in government would not lose touch with its members and that a culture of betrayal could not develop in the grassroots" has plainly been thwarted, on both counts. There are other ghostly echoes of Euro-communism, in the 1996 proposals for a "University for Labour" (whatever happened to that?) which harks back (without attribution) to the 1970s Communist University of London, or for *"turning Labour branches into agents for social change and community regeneration"* on the CP's latter day, looser 'democratic centralist' model. And more broadly, there is shrinkage of historical analysis and political strategy into lists of discreet and unrelated 'policy objectives' within the conventional categories of government (or rather, that other New Labour buzzword for the 'profession' of politics, 'governance').

The journal *Renewal* was founded "*to promote the underlying politics of modernisation to a wider layer of activists, academics and opinion formers*" and fill "*a very particular gap in the market for a non-sectarian but clearly focused and intellectually rigorous journal for Labour modernisers*".[54] There are more echoes here of *Marxism Today*. It hired the same designer as *MT*, but weirdly *Renewal* ended up looking and sounding much more like the earlier, pre-Jacques 'journal' edited by James Klugman, dry and dull in content and staid in design and layout, another 'shrinkage' perhaps (Neal Lawson says it was trying to look like *New Left Review*). Within the politics of the emerging New Labour project, "*with Blair so far ahead*" (Thompson and Lucas), *Renewal* and associated initiatives represented an attempt by the LCC to get back in front. If so, it was largely in vain. Blair and Co.'s "superhuman" drive and "electrifying" fervour carried all before them, at least till their second year in government, when 'reality' began to exert a brake on what was always an extraordinarily narrowly based and inherently cautious project (or rather, as I argued earlier, faction, with more than a hint of Leninist vanguardism in its political practice). New Labour had 'hegemonized' the Labour left and the broader party, primarily through the 'dizzying' device of 'new times'-era political disorientation, but failed utterly to hegemonize the country or even the political system.

---

[54] P. Thompson & B. Lucas, *The Forward March of Modernisation*, p. 14

The LCC was disbanded in that same year of 1998, observing of itself that *"Even the name Labour Co-ordinating Committee confines us to a previous era"* (Martin Jacques made the same point about the name *Marxism Today* in its farewell issue seven years earlier!), and of New Labour that *"the project is to define a project"*. Neal Lawson puts it rather differently: *"We got elected in 1997, and within a few days we were asking what on earth we do now"*. On this account, the entire subsequent post-landslide period has been a matter of the remnants of the Labour left seeking an answer to that question: what to do, in Neal Lawson's recent more explicitly Leninist terms, with *"state power"*. *Renewal* was absorbed into the outer circle of the governing New Labour camp, on the same 'critical friend' basis that LCC had adopted towards the Kinnock leadership. Amongst its own initiatives was *"Nexus, Britain's first virtual think tank of academics, writers and policy wonks and explicitly committed to New Labour"*. According to Tony Blair, addressing a joint Nexus/*Guardian* conference 'Passing the Torch' on 1st March 1997, *"Nexus has a crucial role in sustaining the momentum of progressive politics."* According to its now sadly untended website, *"Nexus has moved. The site has been archived to provide a record of our work"*, but there is no link provided. [55] Britain's *"first virtual think tank"* seems to have disappeared into the ether. According to its founder, *"Nexus was another Lawson venture... it just tailed off, because it wasn't a politics rooted in anything vaguely left wing."*

---

[55] www.netnexus.org

## Compass Today

*Renewal* continues publication, with a recent 're-launch' and a circulation of around 700, but its impact and 'influence' is limited. There is a close but ill-defined relationship with Compass, which more boldly embodies the LCC's historic role as *"outriders for change"* within the Labour Party. The idea for Compass emerged after the 2001 general election, amid growing disillusion with Blairite New Labour. According to Neal Lawson, *"We were New Labour's best friends, they're going off the rails, let's do something that says we need to get it right."* It is funded *"pretty evenly between members, trusts who can give money to such a political organisation, and trade unions"*, though the trade union element is declining as Compass becomes more critical of government and, by Lawson's admission, less able to procure *"short term deals"* (though not for all: for its campaign against Royal Mail part-privatisation, which – for Lawson – represents *"a pretty serious breach of the labour and social democratic intent of the party"*, Compass has received substantial funds from the Communication Workers Union).

In broader terms, Compass provides (for Neal Lawson)

> *an organised centre of politics founded on equality, democracy and sustainability or new issues like well-being... Compass has become a very strong pole within the Labour Party, centre left, soft left, democratic left, call it what you want. And we're shifting as an organisation, from being a Labour Party oriented group into something that looks as much outside. You have to try to build*

> *organisations that push politicians in the direction you want them to go in... Sometimes I think we're the monks in the monastery in the dark ages, and the job is to keep the flame flickering, then sometimes I think wow look at all these fantastic opportunities for a new politics. The most important trait in any political movement is perseverance.*[56]

This is persuasive stuff; we all need 'optimism of the will', as well as our customary 'pessimism of the intellect'. As such it's an attractive retread of what drew elements of an earlier political generation to the briefly 'Euro'-Communist Party of the mid-1970s. When Neal asks

> *How do you build alliances and networks of people who want social justice, sustainability, greater democracy, proper civil liberties? That's the space we want to work out of. What are the mechanics of joining people up into a progressive alliance? What's the structure, the culture, how do you build confidence and trust so those alliances become more effective? We can work with loads of different people to shape the intellectual and organisational terrain...*

he could be paraphrasing the bolder sections of the 1977 revision of *The British Road to Socialism*, the most thoroughly democratic of the CP's

---

[56] The self-revealing 'mediaeval monk' metaphor recurs in other accounts of the contemporary democratic left; David Purdy describes his role with Democratic Left Scotland – which has survived the 2000 disbandment of the CPGB's successor UK-wide organisation and produces a lively magazine *Perspectives* – as "illuminating manuscripts" (personal conversation).

programmes, right down to the use of quasi-Gramscian political metaphors like 'space', 'mechanics' and 'terrain'.[57] The concept of a "progressive alliance" is very close to the 'anti-monopoly alliance', or latterly the 'broad democratic alliance', with which the CP sought (and persistently failed) to break its political quarantine.

And when Neal says, in justification of Compass' commitment to Labour, *"you have to capture state power in order to give power away and do all the things you want to do"*, he's not very far away (given the intervening 32 years of demoralisation and retreat) from the 1977 *BRS' "the essential feature of a socialist revolution is the winning of state power"* (as well as a similar vagueness about what you actually do with it).[58] When he adds *"But that's not enough, you have to build up civil society as well if you really want to take on conservative vested interests"*, he could be tabling a Euro-communist amendment in the bright-eyed manner

---

[57] I am grateful to Sally Davison for pointing out this historical resonance. The *BRS* was only partially democratised in 1977; it contained surprisingly large residues of earlier Communist perspectives, formulations and slogans. The mainstream Euro-communists, the self-styled "revolutionary democrats", consoled themselves that it was at least "a step in the right direction", while more established dissidents David Purdy and Mike Prior derided it as "shoddy tinkering" and left the party soon afterwards; G. Andrews, "Intellectuals and the Communist Party Leadership", in *Opening the Books*, p. 240. Jon Cruddas MP also makes much use (when he's not spinning entertaining and enlightening political fables about various "mates of mine") of 'Gramscian' terms like "contesting the political terrain", speech to Compass AGM, 14th November 2009.
[58] CPGB, *The British Road to Socialism* (London 1978), p. 36

of the year-long 1977 *BRS* debate, memorably recorded in a Granada TV documentary, *Decision: British Communism*. Likewise, you could easily adapt the 1977 *BRS* formulation *"Ready to listen and learn as well as provide strategic leadership, Communists will more and more become a trusted and respected popular force"* to describe Compass political strategy for its own 'long march' through the Labour and parliamentary institutions.

If the LCC (described now by Neal Lawson *"as a funnel to inject new ideas into the Labour Party"*) adopted the broader historical perspective and social analysis of Euro-communism (eventually!), then Compass seeks to apply the CP 'Euro' current's practical politics of alliance-building, policy 'intervention' and strategic 'leadership'. But there always was immense conceit and self-aggrandisement in that last notion, of a small intellectual current within a tiny marginal party purporting to lead a complicated modern nation-state. And in the same way that British Euro-communism lacked the means to actually impose any of this on bigger political forces and historical circumstances (including the CP itself, with all its "historic baggage"), so Compass – while much 'admired' and 'respected' in and around the Labour Party – actually achieves very little for all its political 'busy-ness'. A policy retreat here, the winning of a 'position' there; Compass is kept respectably oppositional, seeking credit by association with populist causes like the bankers bonus tax or resistance to Royal Mail part-privatisation.

We 'happy few' Euro-communists also made very nice political friends and advisers, but were very rarely admitted into real positions of leadership, the 'smoke-filled rooms' and the 'corridors of power' of British politics. The best we could hope for, like Compass now, was a glimpse through a slightly open door, or flattering condescension from the real power-brokers. And, I repeat, all our "revolutionary democratic" insights and "new times" perspectives were reduced, cherry-picked and neutralised along the way. Neal Lawson admits to having *"drawn inspiration from going to the Marxism Today events in the '80s, and styled successive things, especially for Compass, around that model"*, but when he says these later Compass events *"were not as cultural as I'd have liked"*, he gives us another historical example of that reduction or 'shrinkage'.

Like 'Gramscian' Euro-communism, the 'democratic left' politics of Compass is easy to admire and difficult to disagree with. But if it didn't work for and in the CP, which baulked at the leap into modern democracy and pretty quickly fell back onto the more familiar 'terrain' of militant labourism with the defeat of the Euro-communists at its 1979 Congress over the party's own internal democracy, why should it work some thirty years later (and in far bleaker political circumstances) for and in the Labour Party? The CP may have been carrying the baggage of Stalinism, economism and workerism and plenty else (including, I've always thought, some very peculiar people amongst its membership), but the bigger party has its own historical burdens (and its very own collection of oddballs and saddos), and even less of an appetite for intellectual debate, the politics of alliance, the reshaping of ideology and culture, and democracy as a principle rather than merely a means to power.

102

While it sits there, with its deadening historical presence and institutional inertia, the prospects for any genuinely transformative political project of the democratic left, inside or outside the Labour Party, remain pretty bleak.

There is a further, even more difficult historical fact about Labour-Communist relationships. Throughout their mutual existence, elements of the Labour left have mimicked the phrases and slogans of the CP. The CP would be duly flattered, and imagine that this indicated a far closer relationship – "left unity" and the potential for "a Labour government of a new type" – than ever actually existed. What the CPGB never fully understood was the process whereby, deployed within the institutional frameworks of the Labour Party and the parliamentary state from which communists were ruthlessly excluded, these rhetorical formulations were domesticated and tamed. What we ended up with was Labour left MP Eric Heffer's *The Class Struggle in Parliament* and Dennis Skinner's House of Commons class-clown act. It got them rave reviews in the *Morning Star* but ridicule everywhere else. The far cannier Italian communists called this kind of thing 'maximalism' – overblown rhetoric with little practical effect – and kept their distance, even from the pro-Soviet but loudly 'maximalist' 'Third International Socialists' of the 1920s.

In Britain very few people ever actually took seriously the 'revolutionary' phrase-mongering and sloganeering of the CP and the Labour left, except those with a vested interest in 'mobilising' or frightening the general population (still an underlying motivation for most public references to 'the left', especially by right wing press commentators), and 'ruling class hegemony' was never substantially threatened. The problem was, and remains, that the Labour Party has never been an appropriate agent of historical change, but rather an object of and obstacle to it. The ultimate test for Compass, for all its commitment to alliance, democracy, pluralism and partnership, and for its viability as a life raft out of the wreckage of Labourism, is whether it allows membership of political parties other than Labour. That is something it has so far refused to contemplate, as I found when I applied as a (not particularly avid) member of the Green Party. Under Labour Party rules, it would expose Compass to what we in the CPGB used to call "administrative measures" within the factional bun-fight of the "political wilderness" of the contemporary Labour Party. And just as I was expelled from the Labour Party in 2002 for sitting (and voting) with the Greens on my local city council, Compass risks expulsion by being associated with any anti-Labour electoral campaign. For as long as that's the case, Compass can only ever claim to have a little toe in non-Labour waters.

At its last AGM, a Compass member rather plaintively asked whether the organisation was "*demographically representative*". What he actually meant was that almost everyone in the room was white (from my vantage-point at the back, I spotted one black face, and she arrived late and left early). But more striking, and politically significant, is the organisation's age-profile (as represented by attendees at its AGM and larger rallies): lots of bright, borderline-geeky young men (and one or two borderline-geeky young women), much taken with the technology on display like the MTV-style video that opened proceedings. Then, and very much dominating the ensuing discussions, was a roughly similar number of very much older people. This was an audience of students and pensioners, 'youngsters' and grandparents, with a 'missing generation' of the middle-aged where – broadly speaking – power and responsibility reside in our politics and society.[59] Compass has plenty of youthful exuberance and experienced seniority, but very little practical, responsible adult clout. Like the broader, historical left, it does not involve the people who actually run things. This says a lot about the all too evident and much commented-upon 'disconnect' between politics and real life.

It also helps to explain the abstraction, detachment and tendency towards empty moralism of Compass publications and 'debates' like "The Good Society", which was the subject of several large working parties and glossy pamphlets, continues to feature prominently on its website, and even (with the aid of *Soundings* magazine) 'went European' in the form of a web-based 'discussion' on the future of social democracy (at a moment when, across Europe, the political agencies of social democracy appear to be undergoing a process parallel to Labour's of disintegration and steep decline). There is no indication that "The Good Society" has had any practical impact on political discourse, but that does not seem to have been its purpose. Rather, it was meant to indicate that Compass could somehow stand above the whole grubby

---

[59] At the Compass 2009 AGM, the first *frisson* of controversy occurred when an older woman remarked that "*young people don't know anything about politics*".

business of parliamentary jostling, media spin and scandal, political corruption and careerism encapsulated in the furore over MPs' expenses; another astute piece of 'brand-positioning' within the labour movement's 'market of ideas', with very little real application to the outside world.

One of the broader functions of Compass, like all of Labour's historical factions, is to enable young, politically-inclined people (mostly men) to form a worldview which they will obdurately carry through the rest of their lives. Even when forced by 'events' to modify or abandon that formative stance, it's still dimly discernible under the surface or in late night bar conversation. Another is to enable very much older people to recall what might have been (a "good society") if their own youthful dreams had been realised, and dream that (with the respectful aid of all these bright youngsters) it might still be. Beyond that, there is very little sign of Jon Cruddas' Labour *"lodestar, changing the world."*

## Postscript 1 - Who Are These People? A New Labour Left Roll-call

At the very end of Lucas and Thompson's *The Forward March of Modernisation* there is a helpful appendix listing the membership of the successive LCC Executive Committees from 1981 to 1998. It's a kind of 'soft left' family tree (and gold dust for historians), which provides some gauge of the organisation's changing priorities and personnel over most of its lifetime. To begin with, in the early to mid-1980s, it's mostly MPs and stalwarts of the National Organisation of Labour Students (NOLS, a key proving ground for modern – and 'modernising' – career Labour politicians; remember those entrained LCC students coming to sink 'the leading role of the working class'). Other interesting names pop up – the Labour historian Eric Shaw, 'gorgeous' George Galloway, Cherie Booth (no sign of her husband), millionaire heiress and future New Labour junior minister (and serial patron of 'democratic left' causes) Fiona MacTaggart – but for the most part these are dedicated party operators and managers, 'behind-the-scenes' people.

In the mid- to late 1980s, there is a brief, small shift towards local government and the heroes of 'municipal socialism', including for just one year Ken Livingstone; then into the '90s, an increase in the proportion of 'advisers' and 'policy wonks', reflecting the rising influence of MPs' staffers and 'left-leaning' think tanks, the pacification of the party under Kinnock's latter day centralisations and consolidations, and a palpable shift between generations and types of Labour 'activists' in these 'new times'. The old combat and donkey jackets make way for sober suits and tasteful ties; beards are trimmed or removed; anti-racist and anti-nuclear lapel badges are replaced by a single, discreet, union or party pin. After that it all seems to settle down, with the same names recurring every year: the formation of a distinctive generation within the political class, self-selecting and self-supporting, preparing themselves and their party for government. These are the professional 'campaigners', fixers and lobbyists, peddlers of 'ideas', policies and 'influence', the 'organic intellectuals' of the modern Labour Party, 'organising' its affairs, debates and public presentations; bright-eyed, smooth-faced, soberly attired, rather one-dimensional men and women.

In their fastidiously researched but deep-dyed sectarian account of the ill-fated but crucially transitional Kinnock leadership, Richard Heffernan and Mike Marqusee lay bare the career path from the Bennite "task force" of the early LCC to New Labour on the verge of government, via NOLS and what became its fiefdom the National Union of Students, and the 'soft left' in the Party machinery, trade union officialdom and the Parliamentary Party leadership.[60] *"These Labour movement arrivistes brought with them a predilection for tight-knit caucus politics, for the deal struck behind closed doors, which they had acquired in student politics, (and) well-honed skills in faction-fighting which were highly valued by the Kinnock leadership."* They were concentrated almost wholly in London, around Westminster and selected boroughs and Constituency Labour Parties, *"a coterie of trainee professional politicians. Value-free, ambitious, convinced of their own inherent right to govern; their only interest in political ideas or political debates was to manipulate them to outflank rivals or promote favourites"*. The political style of New Labour – what Compass at its best is desperate to leave behind – is all too evident in this caricature.

There are other historical continuities. For all its early distaste for "MP fan clubs", the LCC always carried a heavy superstructure of inactive 'names' and notables (just as the CPGB cultivated a layer of

---

[60] R. Heffernan & M. Marqusee, *Defeat from the Jaws of Victory*, pp. 166/184

celebrity 'sympathisers'), as well as its core activist cadre of what Heffernan and Marqusee call *"NOLS insiders, straight out of student politics with little practical Labour Party experience"*, or for that matter of life in the larger world. Compass shows this same propensity for a layer of left wing celebrities on its conference platforms and publicity: the music journalist John Harris, often accompanied by friendly pop stars looking to be taken seriously (and if they're not available, Billy Bragg), the ubiquitous Polly Toynbee and Baroness Helena Kennedy QC, and other members of *"the wider progressive community"*.

LCC literature, according to Heffernan and Marqusee, was *"peppered with enigmatic injunctions: 'ideals need ideas'... 'articulate the alternatives'"*. These would find an echo, in style and (lack of) substance, in Compass' later motto, supposedly a quote from Ghandi, 'Be the change you wish to see in the world' (did they mistake it for something by near-namesake Gramsci?). Other more resonant, handily shorthand but not hugely meaningful formulas – developments of the classic New Labour 'soundbite' – recur in Compass commentary: *"New Labour inverted the logic of social democracy, to make the people serve the market"*, *"New Labour was neither new nor Labour enough"*, *"a transformed Labour Party is necessary but not sufficient"*. And like LCC (and New Labour in government), Compass leaves behind a litter of abandoned campaigns, slogans and projects which briefly flash across the political/media stratosphere, generate much favourable newspaper coverage, and leave no lasting trace but a vague sense that these people are 'players'.

Heffernan and Marqusee conclude their account of the LCC with a list of their own, of dozens of NOLS/LCC activists who would go on to make their careers (and lives) in and around the Labour Party. By 1997, the year of New Labour's landslide general election victory, (according to another analysis) fully 27 per cent of the party's new intake of MPs described themselves occupationally as *"political organisers".*[61] The proportion in 2010 is even higher, with every declared party leadership contender (except 'maverick' Diane Abbott) having been a political adviser to senior MPs. This represents a new curriculum vitae for Labour, displacing earlier generations of pre-war trade unionists, post-war public sector professionals (all those Croslandite lecturers and managers), then under Thatcher, lawyers and another whiter-collared influx of trade union officials and local government officers. They all at least had some prior experience of life outside the Parliamentary Labour Party. The New Labour generation have brought with them the rather narrower life-experiences of bitter faction-fighting in student, party, council and trade union politics; but precious little sense of life's broader setbacks and consolations. These are the 'child-soldiers' and 'robots' you see drafted in to by-election campaigns or cheering the arrival of a Labour minister at some conference or PR stunt. Or, seemingly from nowhere, becoming one of those Labour ministers...

Heffernan and Marqusee's is a thoroughly jaundiced account, an embittered funeral oration for the Labour 'hard left', but it contains an

---

[61] P. Johnson, *Daily Telegraph* 11th May 2009

important kernel of truth about the way in which modern Labour goes about its business: it is, to say the least, dull and remorseless, with regular outbursts of unpleasantness and personal acrimony, and very little time for the bigger issues of political theory, principles and ideas. There is a harsh, impatient focus on the processes of politics rather than its purposes, on means over ends, objectives over aims, the immediate over the long term, personalities over 'policies', insults over 'issues'. Labour has an abiding tendency to reduce big ideas to fit its own small political horizons, primarily by the exclusive focus of its inner life on the winning 'by any means necessary' of formal policy debate and elected office, which requires shifting coalitions of convenience around certain fixed 'lines' and 'positions' and the constant exchange of personal favours and obligations. And always the debilitating question, central to the age-old empiricist Labour reflex, and foreclosing further or wider 'debate': "*And what are you going to do about it?*" To which the answer always seems to be (even in the leftist Labour Representation Committee's 2010 post-mortem): "Join the Labour Party."

This style of politics can be found all across the 'broad church' and at every stage of Labour history, but in earlier times it was relieved by some level of intellectual ferment, and leavened by rituals of humility and deference, a protective and solidaristic "*ethos*" derived from the proletarian experience of subaltern resistance to capitalist exploitation.[62] MPs granted their grateful

---

[62] H. Drucker, *Doctrine and Ethos in the Labour Party* (Edinburgh 1979)

constituents regular 'interviews' (this was the term for what are now called 'surgeries'), and were duly 'returned to Westminster' with thumping majorities that 'you might as well have weighed as counted' and that (as in parts of Hugh Gaitskell's South Leeds constituency) were summoned to vote street by street by Labour officials ringing hand-bells.[63]

Those rules and manners of 'respectable' interpersonal relations have now been stripped away in the acid bath of cultural populism. You won't find too many of Gaitskell's *"simple honest souls"* or much of Tony Crosland's *"uninhibited mingling"* in the modern Labour Party (or, for that matter, very much original thinking).[64] This kind of politics also attracts and produces a certain kind of personality, on a spectrum from the quietly diffident, through the meticulous 'nit-picker' to the crashing bore. These are not particularly bright sparks, but oh how they would like to be, which partially explains their admiration for *Marxism Today* and the 'Euro-communists', who could be just as shallow and narrow and factionalist, but numbered among them some genuine intellectual 'stars' and carried the inverted, semi-clandestine historical glamour that came with the burdens of CP membership or association.

## *Postscript 2 - No Turning Back?*

One of the fullest recent statements of the Compass 'position' came in a *New Statesman* article by Neal

---

[63] A. Pearmain, "Hugh Gaitskell: How He Came to South Leeds", available from andrew.pearmain@uea.ac.uk
[64] P. Williams, *Hugh Gaitskell* (London 1979); S. Crosland, *Tony Crosland* (London 1982)

Lawson and John Harris in March 2009.[65] It was called "No Turning Back" for no obvious reason; one of those *"enigmatic injunctions"* which Heffernan and Marqusee found in the works of the LCC, perhaps, and which could be readily adopted by any of Labour's wings and factions. In the same vein, the article begins: *"we have to change completely the way we live."* Well yes... Its diagnosis of political crisis is hard to fault: *"there is a grim sense of business as usual"* and *"a very dangerous disjunction between the actions of career politicians and the aspirations of wider society"*; *"Labour still genuflects to the forces of big business"*, and the party's responses to social and environmental emergency amount to *"little more than cynical window-dressing"*. The most coherent response from within Labour has been *"a revival of pre-Thatcher politics"* (Ah, so that's what we're not supposed to turn back to...) but that won't do: *"we need green jobs, not jobs at any cost"* and *"If there is to be no turning back to market fundamentalism, there can be no turning back to state and party fundamentalism either."*

So far, so *Marxism Today;* a manifesto for the New Labour left which Compass seems to want to represent. There is even a nod towards the 'Gramscian sociology' of Karl Polanyi (which I and my fellow-authors of recent neo-Gramscian text *Feelbad Britain* made fertile use of) in Lawson and Harris' *"To turn society in a different direction, markets will have to be regulated and trammelled by social forces – the state and civil society... institutions that allow society to make the*

---

[65] *New Statesman,* 5th March 2009

*market its servant.*"[66] The problems start – just as they always used to in *Marxism Today* – when we turn to what strategic action to take about it all, and get whole fistfuls of crumbs of comfort and grasped-at straws. So, "No Turning Back" offers "hints of something better" in the machinations of *"left Brownites"* and *"new progressives"*, while *"the TUC are making daring noises"*. Meanwhile, a long way from the Labour Party, there is the *"growth of social movements, many with an international focus"* (and as such surely symptoms of the 'national' political left's decline), *"and millions of ordinary people doing what they can to change their lives and make those of others better – by buying ethically, recycling, volunteering and downshifting"* (we all must do what we can, but these are personal ameliorations not political challenges, and for all that 'the personal is political' there is a crucial and profound distinction between our daily lives and party politics). Then we're onto the weary, quasi-New Labour mantras of *"single issues have to be joined up"* and *"a politics that transcends tribal party lines"*.

The online discussion (admittedly not often a source of good sense) of the *NS* article was largely along the sceptical lines of the above paragraphs. "No Turning Back" offers us a compelling analysis of the crisis in British politics, but absolutely no sense of what to do about it, especially in and around the ailing Labour Party of which Compass remains such a resolutely 'loyalist' faction. The article rather gives the game away with its concluding ten policy points, of which (according

---

[66] P. Devine, A. Pearmain & D. Purdy, *Feelbad Britain* (London 2009)

to Neal Lawson) *"nine were in the Green Party manifesto in the 2005 general election, about six were in the Liberal Democrats' and none of them were in the Labour Party manifesto."* The party 'machine' shows no sign of willingness to incorporate Compass 'policy points' into the 'official' party line, or gratitude for Compass' precious life-support. Meanwhile, "No Turning Back" co-author John Harris wrote more recently in the *Guardian* that he was giving the Labour *"dinosaur"* another year or so, before emulating most of his friends in voting, supporting or even joining the Greens.[67] We don't know what he did at the recent general election.

One of Neal Lawson's recent public utterances, in response to Labour's terrible performance at the Norwich North by-election, included the quite bizarre observation that *"this is a centre left moment"*.[68] There was no supporting argumentation, when all the electoral evidence – with the victorious Tories and UKIP combined out-polling every other party, and Labour reduced to whispering that the Tory candidate was a lesbian (she isn't) – points in a different direction, to a 'centre-right moment'; just like the outcome of the general election. The response of the entire political-media class to the onset of recession in 2008 – the absolute, unquestionable necessity of shoring up bank balance-sheets at the expense of an entire generation's employment prospects, and the gathering storm of similarly 'inevitable' but ideologically driven and economically perilous public spending cuts – testify to the continuing

---

[67] J. Harris, *The Guardian* 30th May 2009
[68] Compass website, comment posted 25th July 2009

stranglehold of Thatcherism on our national-popular common sense. Whatever it is, this is most definitely not "a centre left moment".

## *Postscript 3 - Which direction now for the 'Democratic Left'?*

There is a very definite sense here of a historical current in Labour politics that has run its course, veered in one direction or another over its thirty-odd years of existence, and now lies becalmed in a comfortable but slowly cooling and evaporating puddle. New Labour is clearly exhausted, though its key personnel are busily constructing for themselves other guises and vehicles inside or outside government. Pretty much everything any of them have been doing for the last few years has been guided (and explained) by the imperatives of 'positioning' after looming general election defeat.

The Labour Party is in worse shape than ever before, and increasingly haunted by the (so far) barely articulated question: what's the point of a Labour Party if there will never be another Labour government?[69] This was after all, amid the muddle of its early 20th century foundation, its clearest original purpose. Its main historical intellectual current, social democracy, foundered on mid-1970s capitalist crisis, and for all the later efforts to 'rethink' and revive it (even in this latest capitalist

---

[69] This was the theme of one of Compass' most recent publications, *The Last Labour Government.* It argued that electoral reform – on a kind of last-ditch, emergency basis, to be approved with a referendum on the same day as a hopefully indecisive 'hung parliament' outcome to the general election – would at least stop any other single party ever forming a majority government.

crisis, with muted forms of 'neo-Keynesianism'), just won't come back to political life. This latest recession, like every other since the mid-1970s, is being resolved at the expense of the working class and the public sector, and to the further benefit of the middle and upper class and private business. Meanwhile Labour's social and cultural roots in the 'national-popular' lived experience of Labourism are breaking up and dispersing with the profound disaffection of its 'progressive' middle class intelligentsia, the continuing disintegration of the British working class and the mutation of some of its nastier pieces into aggrieved howls of reaction like the BNP.

In late 2009 Compass held one of its 'rallies' with the Communication Workers Union against part-privatisation of the Royal Mail, in my home city of Norwich. I went along, partly to say hello to Neal Lawson but also for the purpose of research for this article. There were 26 people in the audience, including me, and fully 8 panellists, 7 men with one female SERTUC official seated behind a sturdy top-table; not much sign of 'new ways of doing politics' here. The trade unionists' speeches were all about Labour government treachery and betrayal, and the union's rousing defiance: "We will continue to fight to keep the Post Office public for the next 300 years!" The SERTUC official began her speech by thanking Henry VIII for the Royal Mail. Lord Mandelson was the communal villain (it's a shame he no longer has a moustache, because we could imagine him twirling it, pantomime-style). A friendly local Labour MP blamed the last Tory government for creating the "*steamroller of privatisation*", and urged us to vote Labour because the next Tory government would use the Labour legislation to proceed from part- to full privatisation. Neal Lawson pledged the continuing support of *"a radical left wing organisation like Compass"*, but urged us to seek the broader support of *"people on the centre left"* on the basis that *"Royal Mail is one of the few places where we are still equal"* because we all pay the same for stamps.

The ensuing discussion was mostly a chance for angry postmen to tell us they'd never vote Labour again, but I couldn't help pointing out (after the MP had made the customary MP's early departure) the profoundly depressing double bind facing the CWU, one of the few remaining unions with a serious corporate presence in their 'industry'. The more vigorously they resisted the government, and the more public support they seemed to be winning, the more determined the government would become to face them down for resisting 'modernisation'. And the 'public', already being whipped into a froth of fury about the supposed privileges of public sector employment – job security and pensions and so on – and the 'inevitability' of public spending cuts to pay for the banking 'bail-out' under the next government (of whatever party stripe), will not side with the posties. This would all be part of the calculations of that most calculating of politicians, Lord Peter Mandelson. If this really was all about the government's ideological commitment to privatisation, and smashing old-style union resistance to it, then the union – no matter how many 'constructive and viable alternatives' Compass and others supplied them with – was on to a loser.

The panellists mostly looked back at me blankly (several approached me afterwards to say yes I was right, it was deeply depressing. They personally had given up on Labour, and they hoped their union was going to disaffiliate). My point about the CWU's double bind seemed to be confirmed when talk turned to the alliance-building required for success, and a union official observed that *"we don't want to be seen to be leading that, because we don't want to give the right wing press ammunition"*. Neal talked rather forlornly again about this being *"a centre left moment"*, which prompted discussion to turn to the desirability of a general strike. Or rather, as a *Socialist Worker* seller contributed from the door, *"a chance to re-fight the miners' strike and win this time..."*

My final thought on leaving the rally was: why is Compass involved so heavily in this? The campaign, for all its carefully marshalled argument and widespread support, is bound to lose in the end, because the Royal Mail is one of the few remaining public services with lucrative functions which can be readily incorporated into the established commercial sector; another example of Thatcherite cherry-picking. Part-privatisation has been delayed by the Labour government's parliamentary travails, and the need to head off CWU disaffiliation before an expensive general election campaign. It has simply been deferred for Cameron to implement, and for the union to gloriously but uselessly oppose, thereby proving the new Tory government's anti-union mettle. I can only imagine Compass' involvement is some kind of payback for the CWU's sponsorship of its conferences and publications, allied perhaps to some calculation of who might be lured on board the Compass life raft after the general election defeat and possible Labour implosion (actually the Greens are better placed to take advantage of union disillusionment with Labour, especially among the still vigorous public sector and ex-public utility unions).

After the meeting in Norwich I found myself thinking, reminded by the *Socialist Worker* seller perhaps, of the 1984/5 miners' strike, and the disastrous double-bind it had forced on the Communist Party. The CP was caught between the industrial syndicalism of Arthur Scargill and the coruscating neo-liberalism of Margaret Thatcher (and the manic egotism of both), between its own 'militant labourism' and its latter day commitment to democracy, with its 'leading comrades' pleading in vain behind the scenes for a national ballot. It was, as it turned out, a significant step along the way to the CPGB's dissolution, as well as the far bigger losses of a tradition of industrial militancy, of solidaristic community and a whole proletarian way of life. Meanwhile, Labour under Kinnock, Smith and Blair set about making itself "electable" again.

The Compass/CWU campaign looked like another inner Labour fix between the brothers and the factionalists, as well as a further chance for Compass to distance itself from the hard core of New Labour ahead of the expected general election defeat and the remaining Labourists' dash for their own life-rafts. Compass was 'positioning' itself as the core of a purist rump, led by chief Labour 'conscience-keeper' Jon Cruddas, which will spend the next few years attempting (and no doubt, in narrow organisational terms, succeeding) to sustain an ailing but comfortably oppositional Labour Party, and coming no nearer a genuinely 'hegemonic' political project than Labour has ever done. And what, as diehard Labourists always counter, is the practical alternative to any of this? Well, bearing in mind the way Labour post-mortems have always gone in the past, with their untypical receptiveness to outside perspectives, and my 'delayed infection' hypothesis, let's ask: what were we ex-Euro-communists saying a few years ago? I seem to remember an article in the Compass-aligned magazine *Soundings* arguing that for any prospect of progressive political change in Britain, of genuine 'realignment of the left' and re-connection with the hopes and fears of ordinary people, "Labour Must Die!"[70] Oh yes, it was me that wrote it...

---

[70] A. Pearmain, "Labour Must Die!" *Soundings 2005*

# Left Out: Policies for a Left Opposition

122

# Searching for the Left

## Michael Prior

### *Introduction*

The left has existed in the parlance of European politics for over two hundred years since the Jacobins sat on the left side of the National Assembly following the French revolution. Ever since, just what defines the left at any given moment and in any particular country has been controversial particularly amongst the left itself, always a notoriously argumentative and fissiparous bunch. This has been particularly true of the British left over the past twenty years to the point where it almost defies definition. This problem will be tackled later. However one thing is clear; in the last thirty years, the British left has been through tough times amounting to humiliation. After defeat in frontal confrontation with a resurgent and radical conservatism under Margaret Thatcher, it has been largely marginalised within its original political formation, the Labour Party.

The primary aim of the Party became electability, so that, in the name of 'modernisation', it adopted the neo-liberal base of Thatcher's politics with a layer of social concern allegedly directed towards improving the lot of the most disadvantaged in society. This layer was shown to be thin and transient just as the great experiment in neo-liberal free-market economics started to collapse in 2007 and as one of its main progenitors, Tony Blair, left the British political scene. As the banks fell into disarray, the stark facts of British society were laid bare. The previous decade of Labour government had been one in which a version of the classic ditty was only too applicable: the rich had had the pleasure whilst the poor had got the blame and were to suffer the pains of recession.

Unfortunately, while the British left was justly able to complete the chorus of "Ain't it all a bleeding shame", it has essentially been paralysed with regard to offering any systematic alternative. Now that Gordon Brown's rudderless administration has stuttered to its closure, the left, some of whom had initially rather placed their hopes in him, stays in the shadows. A new kind of government, a coalition between two parties has appeared, which may or may not prove stable over the full lifetime of a Parliament. Meanwhile, the left does not appear to have any coherent response to the political crisis, a crisis essentially of legitimacy made all the more serious because it overlaps with an economic crisis.

Various concerns including constitutional reform have popped up on the left as issues in much the same way as they appeared on the agendas of Brown and Cameron, as knee-jerk responses, not something springing from any previous belief. Just over thirty years ago, I wrote[71]:

*It is nearly always possible for contemporary observers to believe that their age is of historic significance, that the choices faced by their society at that moment will determine its future for years to come. And, nearly always, such*

---

[71] M. Prior and D. Purdy, **Out of the Ghetto**, Spokesman, Nottingham, 1979 ISBN 085124 245 6 also at www.hegemonics.co.uk/docs/OutOfTheGhetto

*self-importance can come to seem ridiculous in the light of actual events. New directions for a society seldom occur with the regularity of a railway timetable and social theory, including Marxist theory, has often tended to look for the arrival of old trains rather than the departure of new ones. Nevertheless this book is written in the belief that the next few years are likely to prove of historic significance for Britain and, in particular, for the left in Britain.*

*The main basis for this assertion is the precipitate decline in the economic and political status of Britain over the last decade. This needs little in the way of illustration. We discuss the reasons for this decline in some detail below. All that is needed here is one conclusion, that the failure of the Labour administration of 1964-70 even to begin its heralded modernisation of British society marked a watershed in British political life. From the moment of that failure, when the belief that a new direction could be found within the framework of the old system gave way to the usual patch-and-pray ad-hocery, the normal processes of British government began a long-drawn out holding operation, a desperate attempt to hold the centre in the face of mounting centrifugal pressure. That this holding operation has been carried out so smoothly is a testament to the extraordinary resilience and adaptiveness of the British ruling elite and to its powers of consensual domination. Yet it has remained a holding operation for all that: a series of temporary expedients that have held off the more open and dangerous forces.*

# Left Out: Policies for a Left Opposition

In 2010, Britain is waking up from a decade of dreaming which has been almost the mirror-image of the 1970s. Instead of economic decline together with industrial and social rebelliousness, we had been told that a new form of capitalism had solved the problems of both cyclical recession and class conflict. 2008 saw the breaking of that dream and we are now in the middle of just such a political holding operation as the Labour government was desperately trying in 1979.

The Cameron/Clegg coalition is clearly a temporary affair judged in terms of 'traditional' British governance and what it may lead to remains unclear. In 1979, our prediction that the succeeding few years would be of *'historic significance'* for the left in Britain would come true in ways that we could scarcely have imagined. The same may be true of the coming era.

This essay attempts to come to grips with the basic problem of just what defines and could unite the British left and how it could organise to become a leading political force in the country. It is organised in two broad parts. The first is historical, something for which no apology is necessary. The left often suffers from a selective historical amnesia, something at least partly responsible for its failure. To appreciate what needs to be done we need to understand from whence we have come. The second part tries to define what the current left encompasses and, tentatively, attempts to lay out some possible future path. This is an ambitious task and one which undoubtedly fails in some respects. However it does endeavour to approach the task in a non-sectarian and constructive way and I hope that criticisms follow the same path.

## Part I: The Left in British history

### Ancient History

As in the rest of Europe, throughout the nineteenth century the central political cause of the left in Britain was that of democratic reform expressed in two forms; the extension of the franchise and the freedom to organise in the workplace. Neither was easily obtained and in Britain they were inextricably mixed. However, there were also two big differences in Britain compared with the general continental experience.

First, in most of Europe, the political left became dominated by a socialist current in the second half of the nineteenth century. For example, the German Social Democratic Party was formed in 1875 and, although technically illegal until 1890, it made steady progress in elections whilst the Italian Socialist Party was formed in 1892 as the amalgamation of two other parties and by 1900 it had a significant parliamentary presence. French socialist parties began in 1879 though they almost immediately began the process of splitting into more or less 'revolutionary' parties. The common feature of all these and other European groups was that they engaged in electoral politics and slowly achieved prominence in their parliaments in the last part of the nineteenth century. In Britain, full manhood franchise was obtained rather later than in much of Europe (not until 1918)[72] and working-class electoral activity in the nineteenth and early twentieth centuries was conducted largely within the Liberal Party. The only significant socialist

---

[72] The first full male suffrage came in France in 1848 and in Germany in 1867.

party in Britain, the Independent Labour Party (ILP), was formed in 1893 but remained a sidelined and largely regional body compared with the so-called Liberal-Labour MPs such as Keir Hardie.

The development of national social-democratic and socialist parties was far from uniform over Europe with the northern European parties generally being stronger than in southern Europe. But Britain lagged most continental countries in the formation of a national, membership-based party.

The second distinguishing feature of the British left was the dominant role of trade unions which throughout the second half of the nineteenth century extended their scope and membership, often in the teeth of state opposition. It was this struggle for democratic reform around trade unions, rather than party politics, parliamentary representation and the extension of the franchise, which dominated left politics in Britain into the twentieth century.

In February 1900, representatives of most of the socialist groups in Britain (the Independent Labour Party (ILP), the Social Democratic Federation and the Fabian Society), met with trade union leaders at the Memorial Hall in Farringdon Street, London. After a debate the 129 delegates decided to pass Hardie's motion to establish "*a distinct Labour group in Parliament, who shall have their own whips, and agree upon their policy, which must embrace a readiness to cooperate with any party which for the time being may be engaged in promoting legislation in the direct interests of labour.*" To make this possible the Conference established a Labour Representation Committee (LRC). This committee included two members from the Independent Labour Party, two from the Social Democratic Federation, one member of the Fabian Society, and seven trade unionists, effectively equal representation for the political and labour wings. The name 'Labour Party' was first adopted in 1906 by the group of 29 MPs who had won election under the auspices of the LRC.

As McKibbin puts it:

> *Its 'object' in 1910 was to 'secure the election of Candidates to Parliament and organise and maintain a Parliamentary Labour party with its own whips and policy' It was a 'federation of national organizations', a loose and ill-defined alliance rather than a coherent party with specific aims.*[73]

Nationally, the Labour Party only acquired individual membership in 1918, after extension of the national franchise finally to all adult males and some women, when something like the existing constitution was adopted. It was only after 1918 that the party began to contest nearly all seats and to systematically oppose the Liberals, the party which had been the main representative of the working class before 1914 and with whom the LRC had concluded electoral pacts. Its success was then meteoric. By 1924, it was able to form a government, albeit as a minority, and by the end of the decade, it had totally eclipsed the Liberals.

This complex organisational process and its sudden rise to power has provided the Labour Party with unusual, though longstanding, features which still define its nature and politics.

---

[73] Ross McKibbin, **The Evolution of the Labour Party**, OUP, 1974 p.1

First, as a federal organisation in which most democratic power is exerted by affiliated bodies whose own individual members have different relationships with their national body, it has always had only a limited role for individual members. A consequence of this has been a persistent inability of positions which commanded significant, often majority, support within the individual membership to determine party policy as expressed within party manifestos.

Second, it has remained true to its original LRC roots in being primarily an electoral body dedicated to providing the Parliamentary Labour Party (PLP), a separately constituted body with its own rules and policy, with members and to electing local councillors. It has had a minimal role as a campaigning body or one with any ambition to the development of any left political culture outside Parliament. As a result, a wider political body of left campaigns and agencies has always existed outside the LP with overlapping membership and various levels of support but with no official relationship to it. It is a provocative but essentially truthful comment that it has always been this loose gathering, a kind of political penumbra, which has provided the LP with the full characteristics of a political party rather than being just an electoral machine.

Third, the trade unions have always had a crucial role inside the LP, usually one that is supportive of the leadership of the PLP and which provides much of the party's money. In McKibbin's words:

> *One of the most highly class-conscious working-classes in the world produced a Party whose appeal was specifically intended to be*

130

*classless. Accepting the Labour Party meant accepting not socialism but an intricate network of loyalties. In return, the Labour Party accepted its members as long as they understood its disciplines and conventions...This was a trade-union code of behaviour; so were the political aims of the Labour Party essentially trade-union ones...Within these limited terms the Labour Party has had reasonable success. If it is objected that it has not served the 'true' interests of the working-classes the answer is that it was never designed to do so.*[74]

One of the abiding features of unions is solidarity, an unquestioning support of other members against external forces. This, translated into political terms, is essentially a kind of tribalism in which support for the party rather than support for some external political principle becomes the main feature of political calculation. This 'tribalism' has become the dominant way of referring to allegiance to Labour. Neal Lawson, leader of Compass, the Labour pressure group, recently expressed this:

*I am part of the Labour tribe. My family comes from the tribe, as do many of my friends. But I fear my tribe is dying. Tribes that don't adapt in the right ways always do. The final days of this election campaign will be critical in deciding whether the Labour tribe is to face extinction.*[75]

---

[74] *ibid*, p.247
[75] http://www.compassonline.org.uk/news/item.asp?n=9313

This aspect of Labour has been most fully analysed by Drucker in his almost anthropological study of the LP as it existed in 1980.[76]

Fourth, the LP was never a socialist party though it contained elements of support for a socialist political programme in its constitution and a proportion of its elected MPs, though possibly not a majority, would always define themselves as socialist.

This odd, hybrid body might have been expected to undergo various kinds of political development into something like the continental pattern if it were not for its remarkable and, at the time, unexpected transformation into a party of potential government, a transformation which, even after the debacle of the defection of the then Labour Prime Minister, Ramsay MacDonald, in 1931, continued without any serious challenge. Labour won only 7.0% and 6.4% of the votes cast at the two general elections of 1910. In 1924, on an extended franchise, its share was 30.7%, just ahead of the Liberals, who were damaged by the bitter feud between Lloyd George and Asquith, and it was able to form a minority government. As a result, this rather strange political formation has continued to dominate left politics in Britain down to the present day without significant alteration to its original form despite the contingent features of its first structure.

---

[76] H.M.Drucker, **Doctrine and Ethos in the Labour Party**, George Allen & Unwin, London 1979  His work follows a classic anthropological pattern in which an outsider (Drucker was American) gains privileged access to an unknown tribe.

## Less ancient history

The most unusual feature of British political life has been its great stability. Continental European socialist parties underwent three great convulsions in the twentieth century after their formation in the late-nineteenth century. The first was the split into at least two parts, nominally Socialist and Communist, in the early twenties after the Russian Revolution; the second was the long drawn-out cataclysm of fascism and military occupation followed by reformation; the third was the collapse of Communism after 1989. The trajectory of these convulsions was, of course, different in each country from Finland across to Portugal. But what most European socialist parties have in common is that each has been formed and reformed, shaped by outside forces which have in many cases effectively obliterated them and then required them to reform under new conditions. They have in this sense a history, something written into them which acknowledges the way in which the world can change and that political formations are not immutable. This has not led, necessarily, to formations which are either effective or comfortable for those on the left. The extraordinary collapse of the French Communist Party, for example, has not yet led to the vacuum left by its departure being filled by other than a sclerotic Socialist Party, though this may now be changing. But, even so, the map of European left-wing political formations remains one which shifts and changes; at the moment, Germany, France and Italy are all sites of a realignment of the left which may have far-reaching consequences.

The exception to the European pattern, of course, is Great Britain where the left has been largely defined by a single political formation, a curiosity in the context of European socialism in that it has been largely untouched by any of the three convulsions. Formed decades after most European parties, it avoided the first simply by chronology. It was established as a membership party only in 1918 long after most of the Continental parties and so avoided any split after the independent formation of the British Communist Party in 1920.[77] There was simply no time to allow for the formation of rival socialist blocs within the LP before the Russian revolution made a choice between different political paths inevitable. The failure of the second great convulsion to impact on the LP is an obvious historical contingency — Britain was never run by nor occupied by fascists or Nazis — whilst the muffled impact of the third resulted from the total political dominance over the left acquired by the LP in the previous fifty years and the absence of any significant Communist alternative.

The mirror-image to Labour's stable position on the left is that of the Conservatives on the right. Great Britain has been for almost a century a two-party state in which power has shifted regularly between them. Indeed if one substitutes Liberal for Labour, this system has dominated British politics since the mists of time. A first-past-the-post (FPTP) electoral system almost guaranteed the electoral impotence of any other parties whilst the 'broad church' posture of both parties, one to the

---

[77] For more than twenty years, this party, far from splitting the main left party strived to affiliate to it.

left the other to the right, however limited in the actual control of the party, has enabled the extremes on either side to be neutralised if not absorbed. The absence, until recently, of any major regional or religious differences outside Ireland important enough to engage with national politics has reinforced this duality. Again this is a significant difference with Continental politics.

The election in May has provided a break with this long-lasting stability. Hung parliaments are not new, occurring in both the 1920s and the 1970s. In both these cases, they marked radical shifts in the political landscape; in 1924, it marked the eclipse of one of the parties which has previously been part of the normal duopoly whilst in 1976, it provided a base for a new ideological position to dominate the political landscape for forty years. Whether the Tory/LibDem coalition marks a similar radical change is yet to be seen.

Labour was never a socialist party in the classic mould of the Second International, even though its 1918 constitution enshrined the famous Clause 4. It inherited the non-conformist conscience of the Liberals, and its leaders owed more to the Webbs than to Kautsky or Bernstein. There was, nevertheless, a strong socialist current among the party's membership, which normally stood to the left – and often well to the left – of the leadership. For decades, the annual party conference was a battleground, as policies supported by the majority of constituency delegates were regularly defeated by trade union block-votes. Yet despite these repeated collisions, the Labour Party managed to avoid damaging internal splits. The breakaway of the ILP in 1931 and the defection of the SDP in

1981 were only serious schisms, and neither broke the two-party system, though by fighting the 1983 election in alliance with the Liberals, the SDP came close, winning 25.4% of the votes cast compared with Labour's 27.6%, at that point the only time since 1923 that Labour had fallen below 30%. That the Alliance only won 23 seats in that election against Labour's 209 showed the manifest unfairness of the British FTTP system. However, this attracted only sectional interest in the height of the Thatcher revolution.

Labour's relative immunity to splits was largely due to the electoral system. Under FPTP, breakaway parties whose voters are thinly spread throughout the country stand little chance of winning seats in a general election, however many protest votes they pick up at by-elections. Moreover, even during the dark days of the 'National Government' formed after Labour's ignominious ejection from office in 1931 and dominated by the Tories, Labour retained important bastions in local government and thus kept its finger-tips on state power. These facts of political life, brutally encapsulated in Aneurin Bevan's jibe that the ILP after splitting from the LP was *'pure, but impotent'*, were reinforced by class sentiment. In the eyes of many trade unionists, splits in the party formed to defend trade union interests and largely financed by the unions were akin to breakaway unions, acts of betrayal that served the class enemy.

Thus, the Labour Party exhibited a curious stand-off: a largely left-wing membership with nowhere else to go confronted a right-wing leadership which relied on trade union block-votes to avoid conference embarrassments, but needed constituency activists to fight elections. The limits of left-right cohabitation were clearly exposed in the impassioned confrontations of the Gaitskell era. After his attempt to remove Clause 4 from the party's constitution was foiled by the left, Gaitskell campaigned against the 1960 conference decision to support unilateral nuclear disarmament, overturning it the following year by getting a couple of unions to change sides.

In a bid to break out of this impasse and broaden its campaign for a socialist alternative to the policies of the Wilson government, the May Day Manifesto group sought in 1968 to build a new left formation that was less attached to traditional party politics. After some initial success, the movement fell apart in the run-up to the 1970 election. As Raymond Williams, a Manifesto editor, later wryly remarked: *'A strategy for common action could survive anything except an election.'*

During the 1970s, the left inside the Labour Party set out to take it over: the Trotskyite *Militant* tendency by building a party within a party, the Campaign for Labour Democracy by means of open networking and dogged committee work. The Communist Party, the main organisation of the left outside the Labour Party, effectively abandoned electoral pretensions and focused on altering the balance of power inside the LP, developing broad left groupings in the unions and in student politics. Although constituted as a broad left they scarcely bothered to conceal the fact that their intent was to change the LP. They proved remarkably effective, launching the careers of several future Labour politicians, including Jack Straw, Charles Clarke and John Reid, and shifting the balance of power decisively to the left in several unions, including the key Engineering Workers.

By the end of the mutinous 1970s,[78] having gained control of both the party conference and the National Executive Committee (NEC), the Labour left proceeded to change the rules of the game. Party members gained a say in the election of the leader and deputy leader, hitherto the province of the PLP, constituency parties gained the power to deselect sitting MPs, and the NEC was charged with ensuring that the party's election manifesto reflected conference policies. Simply to state these reforms is sufficient to suggest the fundamentally undemocratic nature of the LP up to this point. One common current misconception is that there was once a kind of golden age of LP democracy which has been eradicated by New Labour. In fact, the reverse is true; if anything before 1980, the central machine exerted even tighter control than today.

Incensed by these reforms, particularly constituency re-selection, 27 MPs on the right of the party resigned the Labour whip and in January 1981 followed the 'Limehouse Four' into the SDP. The chief beneficiaries were the Conservatives. Buoyed by military victory in the Falklands and facing a divided opposition at home, Mrs Thatcher was returned to power at the General Election of 1983 with an overall majority of 144, despite receiving only 42.4% of the votes on a turnout of 73%.

---

[78] A good deal of commentary on this decade can be found at www.hegemonics.co.uk

At this point the British left fell apart. There had been no great dissension on the left in the 1970s. A few dissident voices were raised against the strategy of 'militant labourism' – ramping up industrial action over wages and pushing Labour policy to the left via the unions – but these fell on deaf ears. There was little dissent from the left's opposition to the Common Market, even though withdrawal had been decisively defeated by the electorate in the 1975 referendum and was probably the most unpopular of Labour's policies after 1979. And across a spectrum ranging from what would now be called the 'soft left' through the CP to the ultra-left, opposition to any form of incomes policy, the only effective left policy to limit inflation, was *de rigueur*. These positions were, of course, strongly contested by the Labour right. Indeed, during the 1983 election campaign, Dennis Healey, the deputy-leader, openly disavowed the party's manifesto commitment to cancelling Trident and refusing to allow the deployment of US cruise missiles.

However, after 1983, the left descended into open civil war, while the right sought to regain control over the party machine and restore relations with the unions. Two issues split the left: Arthur Scargill's suicidal attempt to take on the Thatcher government, and the government's assault on the powers of local authorities. The NUM debacle blew away what remained of the trade union broad left, as even many Communist activists demurred at Scargill's tactics. The introduction of rate-capping and the abolition of the Greater London Council, along with the other metropolitan councils, was part of a general drive by the Conservatives to impose monetary and fiscal control and raised basic democratic questions about the independence of local government. Councils throughout the country were affected, but the front line was in Liverpool, where the *Militant*-controlled council seemed determined not to set a balanced budget. In the event, *Militant* and the Labour leadership spent more time squaring up to each other than attacking the government, squandering the chance to rally resistance to the neo-liberal revolution at a time when public attitudes to it were still malleable.

The existence of strong Labour-controlled councils had always been a source of great strength for Labour even in the darkest days of the 1930s after the MacDonald defection. The failure of the Labour opposition to defend adequately the role of local government when it was attacked by Thatcher and the subsequent failures of New Labour to restore its lost authority has been a key, if subterranean, factor in the decline of the Labour party.

The main reason for the left's failure to oppose Thatcher more effectively was that it had no hegemonic project of its own. Indeed, it had no political strategy at all beyond the pursuit of 'militant labourism', at root a syndicalist conception of politics, which had already been discredited in the 1970s, when inflation accelerated, tension mounted and profits plunged. Two further, subsidiary factors contributed to the left's decline: the collapse of the CP, as rival factions battled for control; and the efforts of the Labour right to 'reclaim the party', a tortuous and clandestine process documented by Dianne Hayter.[79]

Once Neil Kinnock had embarked on a purge of the *Militant* group, it proved relatively easy to roll back the 1979 reforms, laying the groundwork for the tightly disciplined and centralised party of the New Labour era. There has been tendency among political analysts to see Labour's travails in the 1980s as redemptive punishment for its earlier transgression in making itself 'unelectable', a keyword in the New Labour lexicon that gave a veneer of sophistication to such demotic coinages as the 'loony left' and the 'longest suicide note in history', minted by *The Sun* and Gerald Kaufman, respectively. In a recent pamphlet, Jon Cruddas, generally regarded as the most left-wing candidate in the deputy-leadership elections of 2007, referred to the '*horrors and wreckage of the early 1980s*', neglecting to mention the issue of internal democracy and the SDP's defection, as if Labour had been the hapless victim of some political Black Plague.

Historical amnesia is a besetting weakness of the left. Until things fell apart under Gordon Brown, those who had at first supported Blair, but later became disillusioned, drew a sharp distinction between the 'modernising' years from 1983 to the death of John Smith, and the 'Blairite' years from 1994 to the accession of Gordon Brown. In fact, all the elements of the centralised control that became New Labour's stock in trade were put in place during the Kinnock years. The neutering of the

---

[79] Dianne Hayter, **Fightback!,** Manchester University Press, 2005

party conference and its conversion into a stage-managed spectacle may have gone farther under Blair and Brown than Kinnock intended or foresaw, but the stifling of debate and the cult of the leader began on his watch.

It is important in understanding the current position of the left to compare the slow dwindling of the socialist left with two campaigns in the 1980s conducted by the largely non-socialist left: the nineteen-year protest against cruise missiles by the women's peace camp at Greenham Common and the opposition to nuclear power.

Emerging from the two movements of the 1950s and 1960s that were not dominated by socialists, namely CND and feminism, the Greenham women survived rough policing, prosecution and vicious vilification in the media. What part they played in getting the missiles removed and the US base closed is open to question, but so far as popular protest goes, they were the last women left standing and in doing so achieved wide publicity and almost iconic status as the only lasting opponents of Thatcher.

The anti-nuclear power campaign of the 1980s came from a different direction, that of the environmental movement which had developed from the late 1960s. It was focused on one specific issue — the expansion of nuclear power, an expansion whose ambitions had ballooned to massive proportions following the oil-price rises in the 1970s. Although the long drawn-out public inquiry over the building of a new kind of reactor at Sizewell eventually decided in favour of the developers, the expert arguments of the protestors did convince most outside observers and although the then state-owned generating company, the CEGB, still clung to a notional plan for nuclear development, in practice the proposals were quietly abandoned.

These two, quite different, campaigns spawned the new forms of left political organisation and action which have become dominant over the past twenty years particularly in the form of environmental activism. They are based on consensus decisions, the absence of leaders and direct personal action, together with sound research into the facts of the particular campaign. Essentially they are inheritors of the anarchist tradition so long overshadowed by the socialist left. These movements can be maddening in their search for consensus and their allergy to structure, but their capacity for mobilisation is proven, even if the results sometimes seem ephemeral.

Thus in the early 1990s, the British left had been effectively smashed, killed largely by its own internal dissension and its failure to move beyond the failed policies of the 1970s. It had been supplanted by two, distinct programmes; that of a 'modernising' group inside the LP which was intent on developing a form of socially-respectable neo-liberalism inside the husk of the LP and, externally, campaigning groups focused particularly on environmental and social issues, which had little knowledge of, or time for, the socialist left as it had been constituted.

## The left under New Labour

The New Labour project led by Blair and Brown was a massive success in terms of maintaining a parliamentary majority for thirteen years — a

143

record for any Labour administration — even if the prospect of extending this by another quinquennial under Brown's premiership has gone. New Labour is now be departing from the scene under the cloud of an economic recession, in the eyes of many exacerbated if not brought on by its adoption of the free-market neo-liberal economic policies of its Thacherite predecessor.[80]

There was a political price paid for this success even whilst it remained in power. First, there was a steady erosion of the Labour vote with five million fewer voting for them in 2005 compared with 1997. Second, the electoral turnout plummeted on their watch dropping by over 11%, suggesting a general disillusion with the whole political process. Finally, Scotland and Wales having been given some measure of devolution by Blair, probably unwillingly, have both drifted steadily away from central control. The explosion of public anger over parliamentary expenses essentially rests upon these underlying changes rather than upon the seriousness of the specific wrongdoing uncovered by the *Daily Telegraph*. The (possibly short-lived) flurry of concern about various kinds of constitutional reform suggest that politicians of various hues have woken up to this political crisis.

It would be wrong to suggest that these shifts were provoked by any kind of leftwing protest; the situation was far too complex for that and the left has been far too splintered. Even so, one defining moment in the Blair regime was the massive anti-war march of 2003 followed by Blair's mendacious

---

[80] Mike Prior, **Beyond Feelbad Britain**, 2009, ISBN 9781-4092-5763-1 This can also be downloaded at www.hegemonics.co.uk

and contemptuous response. This moment clarified what had become increasingly clear in the previous decade; that the Labour Party under its new leaders was set upon making a long transition from being a party of the British left to one embedded in the English centre with an inclination to the right. This shift is sometimes presented as no more than a necessary re-adjustment of policy given the obvious electoral cliché that obtaining an electoral majority depends upon a majority of the 'centre' vote. This ignores the fact that the meaning of 'centre' in political terms depends upon the dominant political hegemony of the time and is not fixed. In the decade after 1979, a political faction, which was probably a minority in its own party at the beginning and was always in an electoral minority, decisively shifted the central hegemonic principle of British politics by a process only possible in the British style of 'elective dictatorship'. New Labour was a process of accommodation to this shift following the failed attempts by the British left to resist it in the 1980s. The current crisis of political legitimation essentially derives from the fact that the two parties which had sustained the system of alternating power have essentially overlapped in their policies.

The two-party system buttressed by a FPTP electoral system has, historically, maintained itself because of its ability to provide, successively, modernising and sustaining governments, that is periods when Labour (and before them, the Liberals) could provide the modernising impetus followed by periods of consolidation invariably provided by the Conservatives. In a sense, Thatcher's victory in 1979 broke this pattern by providing a new kind of 'modernisation' with

Labour in 1997 acting as the consolidating force. The Conservative dilemma since then was to become some kind of modernising force without having any of the ideological equipment on which to base this. Cameron's rather loopy attempts to flesh out a Big Society or some such in order to heal Broken Britain exemplified this confusion and almost lost him an election which he should have won comfortably.

The dilemma remains within the fabric of the coalition and will give rise to stresses which may yet cause its collapse. On the other hand, the performance of contenders in the Labour leadership election suggests that they too have little idea how to cope with the transformation of the previous style of British governments. In an odd way, they seem concerned to present themselves both as modernisers but also as traditionalists, a political circus trick clearly well beyond their presentational skills.

One of their principal problems is that, as suggested above, the LP had had since its foundation, a progressive left 'penumbra' around it which furnished the trappings it lacked to be a full political party rather than an electoral machine. The collapse of the left in the LP after the mid-1980s had been paralleled by a similar decline in this external penumbra and the growth in a set of progressive forces that had little or no allegiance to socialism and its groups and very little faith in the electoral process. This can be seen as the NGOing of the left with these campaigning bodies forming the basis for such popular mobilisation as exists around environmental or social issues. Any new

Labour leadership lacks this context within which they can proclaim their new purpose.

It is the context which is important, specifically three issues; the diminished status of trade unions; the loss of moral leadership by the left; and the hollowing out of the British state with the associated crumbling of the two-party system.

The dominating presence of the unions in British left politics has always been one of the defining features of British socialism separating it from the Continental European tradition in which unions have had a supportive but not decisive role. They have had two, distinct and in some ways contradictory roles.

The first was as a politicising agent in the working class in terms both of strengthening support for the party, which it had had a major role in founding, and of providing a steady flow of leaders, albeit largely white males, at all levels of left formations. The negative side of this presence was a persistent strand of syndicalism in these formations, a strand which continued through to the reliance on industrial action to achieve political ends in the 1970s and, ultimately, to the disastrous miners' strike.

The second presence was as part of the bureaucratic apparatus of the LP which, throughout most of its history, sustained a leadership to the right of the majority of the membership. Inside both the national conference and the National Executive Committee, it has normally been the union votes which have kept the party safe for the leadership[81] whilst in the mid-1980s it was union-leaders who restored right-wing authoritarian leadership of the LP and have subsequently backed all the constitutional changes depriving the membership of any role in forming party policy.

These two presences have often been contradictory but, until the last two decades, the first has always been seen by the left as a factor which outweighed the second given that it seemed as though overcoming the ruling right-wing bureaucracy was possible based upon the grass-roots support of a politicised union movement. From the mid-1960s onward for some twenty years, this possibility was the dominant and ultimately successful project within most left groups both within the LP and outside it. Forty years on, this dual-role has been splintered. The unions are, numerically, much diminished. Their previous grip on large parts of the private-sector has all but disappeared and continues to decline whilst their membership is ageing.[82] Union density is now amongst the lowest in Europe. This is a long-term trend begun in the Thatcher years but which has continued unabated throughout the whole period since 1997 under Labour.

That this is a tragedy for British workers is undoubted. However, the political implications of

---

[81] The late-1970s when this normality disappeared was, of course, literally the exception which proved, that is tested, the rule.

[82] In 2006, union density amongst all workers was 25.8% with 17.2% density in the private sector. Union membership was 24% amongst employees aged 25-34 years and 39% amongst employees over 50 years old. This marks a decline from a peak union-density of 55% in 1979.

this long-term decline have yet to be assimilated —
at least on the left for it is clear that Brown and
Blair had long taken them onboard. Essentially, the
second presence, that of providing bureaucratic
support for Labour leaders, remains largely
undiminished. The twelve union nominees to the
Labour National Executive Committee supply
enough reliable votes on their own to provide the
five government nominees with a simple majority
out of thirty-three members leaving the six
representatives of the membership to offer token
dissent. However, the other presence of providing
politicised leadership has almost totally vanished.
Any left project which involves an element of
shifting the unions to the left has effectively
disappeared as they have adopted an increasingly
administrative role with respect to their members.
Essentially, the previous role of the unions as
politicising agents amongst the working class has
largely disappeared.

A significant part in this has been the successive
amalgamations which have left the union
movement dominated by a couple of huge unions
whose internal procedures are tightly controlled by
their central leadership. The lively political debate
at union conferences which fed through to policy
debate at the LP conference has now largely gone.
This is not to suggest that unions never play a
progressive role. In mobilisations against the BNP,
for example, local and regional union offices have
provided valuable support. But, overall, it is clear
that the kind of support for the left which once
existed at grass-roots level has largely disappeared.
Blair and Brown understood this. They knew that
the unions, nationally, are tied to supporting the
Labour leadership in the hope, almost totally

unfulfilled, that they will enact forms of labour legislation which relax the constraints of the Thatcher era. They also know that the left-turn inside the unions of the 1970s will never happen again.

Unfortunately, this obvious fact has yet to dawn on, for example, the CLP representatives on the NEC who campaign vociferously against any action which they see as altering the federal structure of the LP even though this structure is the very thing which renders them impotent. The future role for trade-unions in the British left is one of the great unspoken issues that the left has dodged. The unions have been the refuge and the hope of the socialist-left since before the formation of the LP. They are no longer and can no longer be that. Just where they fit in left politics is unclear but one thing is clear — that the left must now find an alternative road.

The second shift in context, the loss of moral leadership by the socialist left, is more subtle but, in its way, more important. In the mid-1960s, the Labour left had a majority amongst the Party's membership and could offer effective opposition to the leadership because it held on to a moral and a broad intellectual hegemony both inside the Party, which the best efforts of right-wing Labour leaders such as Crosland and Gaitskell failed to dent. This was best seen in Gaitskell's efforts to remove Clause 4 from the party constitution, something supported by a 'modernising' faction within the party which included the young Tony Benn yet to begin his long leftward march.

It was this moral authority rather than any degree of internal democracy which enabled explicit socialists such as Bevan and even near-Communists such as Zilliacus to become MPs and even leaders within the party.

This dominant socialist hegemony also existed outside in a broader left. This domination was based around 'socialism' as it was then understood. In Eley's words: *"For roughly a century between the 1860s and the 1960s, the socialist tradition exercised a long-lasting hegemony over the Left's effective presence...If the Left was always larger than socialism...socialist parties also remained at their indispensable core."*[83] Eley writes of the European left. In Britain, most of the membership of the LP plus that of the Communist Party was the essential core of that broader Left even though the Labour was never a socialist party as such.

By the end of the 1990s, this central hegemony of socialism as the normal language of the left and as a sheet-anchor on the ultimate practice of Labour leaders had disintegrated. Again in Eley's words: *"Socialist languages of politics, socialist models of organising the economy, socialist projections of the good society, socialist ideas in general have all been catastrophically delegitimized...Socialist ideas now have a more embattled and less legitimate place in the public discourse than one might ever have anticipated even two decades before."*[84]

I am not arguing here that this is a good thing but simply stating a fact about the place which the

---

[83] G. Eley, Socialists and the Tasks of Democracy, p.4
http:www.isj.org.uk/index.php4?id=86#content
[84] *ibid,* p.11, http:www.isj.org.uk/index.php4?id=86#content

socialism, which was the core ideal of LP membership in the 1960s, now has in political discourse even on the left. It has no pull, even a residual one, on the Labour leadership, who are now evidently free to pursue whatever policy seems most fitting their own designs, and it has little attraction within a wider activist left. Yet, and this is something that becomes startlingly obvious as one moves around the various public debates centred on the LP, the left within that party seems largely oblivious to this fact. The problem for them remains that of getting back lost members and decrying the betrayal of socialism by New Labour.

The pull of the old socialism certainly varies across the LP left. The much-diminished Campaign group in Parliament led by John MacDonnell together with his support group, the Labour Representation Committee still cling to socialism as such though without being too specific as to what this means. The centre left of the Compass group and its parliamentary hope, Jon Cruddas, display the consistent wavering which might be seen as the hallmark of that uncomfortable political stance. Cruddas and Neal Lawson, Compass' intellectual guru, refer back as much to Tawney as to any socialist texts whilst they often prefer amorphous attacks upon such as 'consumerism' as any direct assault upon capitalism *tout court*. However, they are also markedly unwilling to give up the nominal robe of socialism. Interestingly, Tawney never had many illusions about the LP blaming the failure of the 1929-31 Labour government:

> *The gravest weakness of British Labour is ...[that] it lacks a creed...It does not achieve what it could, because it does not know what it*

*wants...This weakness is fundamental. If it continues uncorrected, there is not nor ought to be, a future for the Labour Party.*

The third shift in context is the one described above, the overall hollowing out of the British state and of the two-party system which has sustained it for so long. This is the issue which is at the heart of the problem of what defines the left and where it resides. In the mid-1960s, Britain was a unitary state governed within the framework of a two-party system, historically largely dominated by the Conservatives but with Labour the only constant and legitimate opposition. Within Labour, there was a socialist left which could visualise itself as being a government-in-waiting. This system has now fallen apart. Scotland and Wales have started down paths of a legal national identity, whose future route is uncertain, but which has already given their nationalist parties a leading role. In England, a slow edging towards a more pluralist political structure had given a third party an increasingly prominent role despite the obvious unfairness of the electoral system. Both Labour and Conservative parties have become almost regional organisations with Labour largely absent from the south and west of England outside London and the Conservatives similarly absent from most of northern England, Scotland and Wales. All this has taken place against a background of growing disillusion with the political system as a whole reflected in the decline in electoral turnout. The May election marks a stage in the disintegration of the old system but only a stage.

These three major shifts in the context of national and party political discourse mean that the 'problem' of the LP is now almost diametrically opposed to that which was posed forty years ago. Then the problem was how to change it internally. Now the problem is how to dissolve its political dominance over the left without provoking a potentially disastrous shift to authoritarian modes of governance and, simultaneously, how to reconstruct the left within a new structure which takes into account the new political landscape of the 21$^{st}$ century.

## *Part II: Searching for the Left*

The long drawn-out historical process outlined in the previous section contains some important conclusions for the British left. Essentially these come down to the fact that for at least seventy years — certainly since the British Communist Party gave up any pretence to achieving power — its political action has been focused on the Labour Party. However, the structure of the LP as a federal body, with only a limited role for individual membership, a constitutionally separate Parliamentary Labour Party and an almost total focus on electoral activity, has meant that this action was largely indirect. Examples of this are the nuclear disarmament campaign in the late-50s and early-60s and the debate around incomes policy in the 70s. In both cases, large-scale action was centred around shifting votes inside constituency Labour parties and union branches which fed through into votes at union conferences and thence into debates at the LP conference which might then feed into government policy. The annual debate at the LP conference became the focus of left activity not just by LP members but by the entire left.

This process climaxed in the second half of the 1970s with the one full-scale attempt by the left to shift the structure of the LP to one dominated not by the Parliamentary party but by the membership. Although initially successful, it ultimately failed for three reasons. First, part of the right-wing of the party defected into an alliance with the Liberal Party. Second, left domination produced a policy

155

which failed to move beyond the 'workerism' of the 1970s. Third (and this is a factor usually ignored by much of the left) it failed to address the crucial question of the role played by the unions inside the LP, one which normally gave unquestioned support to bureaucratic and conservative forces inside the party. The left swing of the 1970s remains a one-off aberration with normal service quickly resuming after 1984.

Things fell apart after about 1985 and the left flowed into channels sufficiently numerous to be regarded as a political delta rather than any countable number of streams.

The most obvious path was to become part of the left diaspora, the large number of people who saw themselves as being on the left, perhaps even political in a general sense, but who abandoned any specific political affiliation. Given initial impetus by the fractious implosion of the Communist Party and expulsions from the Labour Party, this flood has with ups and downs continued to the present as the Labour left has slowly abandoned their party. Highlights in this procession would include giving up Clause 4, the election of Labour in 1997 — which saw a significant number rejoining the LP — the Iraq war and all the subsequent cover-ups which for many marked the final moral decay of New Labour.

Many of those who left formal political affiliation contributed to an important shift in institutional politics, what I called above the NGOing of the left. As the political penumbra of the LP fell apart, its campaigning role shifted more and more into the NGOs which began to play an increasingly important role from the 1980s onward. These included large charities such as Oxfam, Shelter and War on Want as well as environmental NGOs such as Greenpeace and Friends of the Earth. Less prominent but more numerous were a mass of single issue groups, some with specifically charitable aims, others with a more diffuse focus and some with specifically local or community bases. Mostly staffed by people on the left, they took increasingly political stances so that in the early 1990s, a group of them even suggested forming some kind of united front to oppose Thatcherism. This idea was soon knocked on the head but their public stance continued. The culmination could be seen in the G20 marches organised by Put People First, sponsored by around a hundred and fifty of such NGOs and a handful of more traditional agents such as trade unions and a complete absence of specifically political bodies such as LP constituency parties or socialist groups.[85]

These NGOs have highly developed processes of policy formation and are astute in their lobbying. However, the political problem is clear. Apart from sometimes being heavily circumscribed by their charity status, their job, apart from direct charitable work, is that of lobbying whatever political formation happens to make up the government of the time. Acting to change governments rather than changing government policy is outside both their remit and their competence. As a consequence, a feature of this left is that it can now show an impressive list of policy alternatives to the neo-liberal agenda which has characterised New

---

[85] A full sponsorship list can be seen at http://www.putpeoplefirst.org.uk/

157

Labour but little in the way of political options to implement such policies apart from posting them to No. 10. One of the features of the coalition is likely to be the way in which these NGOs switch their attentions to the new government, possibly with rather greater success than under Brown given the need of the LibDem component to show its credentials and the overall need of Cameron to demonstrate some social direction.

The second move has been into other political groups and parties. Some of these are explicitly on the left such as Plaid Cymru, which describes itself as supporting *"decentralised socialism"*, but mostly they contain more or less important left currents such as the Green Party and the Scottish Nationalist Party. There has also been a rather surprising proliferation of successors to the Communist and Trotskyist groups of the 1970s. There seem to be at least ten parties with the words 'Communist' or 'Socialist' in their names and several other groups claiming some form of socialist allegiance.

Finally, there remain those stubborn left-wing members of the Labour Party who hang on, sometimes rather precariously, to the old allegiance. It difficult to discern just how many these number but recent voting patterns offer a clue. Some 53% of the individual membership of the LP took part in the Deputy-Leader election in 2007, that is around 95,000. Of these, 23,000 voted for John Cruddas, the centre-left's standard bearer, in the voting round before his elimination. This voting pattern suggests that although left-wing members of the LP are significant they do not number anything like a majority of individual membership.

These numbers were confirmed when, in a subsequent internal election, Ann Black, supported by the leftwing Labour Representation Committee, obtained 20,203 votes when she was elected to the 2008 National Executive as an individual member. So, perhaps, around 20,000 people whose politics are left of centre were then remaining in the LP. The number has probably dropped since then.

Meanwhile, alongside this left, most of whom would probably label themselves as 'socialists' or at least 'social-democrats', there has developed what I have heard called the 'horizontal left'; those political activists who have given up on the 'vertical left', that is a left organised in any kind of hierarchy and focused on electoral activity, and have formed loose-knit campaigning groups focused on environmental or anti-globalisation issues. Ideologically, the dominant strand in these groups is a form of anarchism rather than socialism, an anarchism which has been stimulated by internet access and ideas about common intellectual property and living outside consumer society. Very smart tactically, knowledgeable, brave and committed, these groups are in a sense the lineal descendants of both the Greenham Women and the anti-nuclear movement of the 1980s. The common feature of what are rather disparate groups is a rejection of modes of organisation which the socialist left has long taken to be required; leaders, hierarchy, decisions taken from on high to low. Instead they have adopted a decision-making process based on consensus and equality. It is true that this intent is often distorted and that personal leadership can be exercised in ways which manipulate the process. But it is also true that these democratic processes emerged as a reaction to the centralised and disciplinarian democracy which many see as characterising the socialist left.

The gap between these activists and the 'political' left is great. The party which might be expected to find most sympathy with them, the Greens, is sometimes seen as co-opted and subservient to electoral processes despite having taken on much of their democratic ethos. Even so in some ways, the Green Party does bridge the gap between the vertical and the horizontal left having, for example, only recently accepted the idea of having a leader rather than spokespeople.

The political problem facing the left is how to bring together these four broad groups into some kind of common action given that the common focus of transforming the LP, which provided a base left unity for many decades, is no longer a feasible option.

## *Where we need to be*

### The problem of culture

The process of political hollowing-out discussed above combined with the catastrophic, if partially self-inflicted, defeats of the 1980s have produced a left in Britain which is scattered, fractious and unable even to recognise itself except by largely meaningless labels of affiliation. In particular and most importantly, the British left lacks any common political culture. This is unusual, even alien, word to use with respect to our politics though it would be understood quite readily in Continental Europe. Culture is a slippery though useful concept in politics. Here I mean, roughly, a body of policies gathered together under the rubric of an over-arching vision of how a future society might look and tied into some kind of organisational mechanism as to how such a vision could be achieved. In order to flesh this out, I want to quote at some length from a previous jointly-authored essay[86]:

> *What might a sustainable post-capitalist world look like? Is it attainable? How long would it take to construct? And how can it be brought closer? How can the majority of people, with daily lives to lead, jobs to do and families and households to maintain, and the usual bundle of personal hopes and worries and preoccupations that we all carry around, embark such a huge, historic undertaking? What use can be made of existing democratic arrangements and political structures? What new arrangements and structures are needed?...How can we create some kind of political agency that is recognisably and coherently green and left wing, while avoiding the horrors, the wasted time and effort, and the sheer tedium of most of what has gone before?*
>
> *These are big questions... We do, however, maintain that these are the right big questions to be asking. Max Weber once said that there*

---

[86] M.Prior, P.Devine, A.Pearmain & D.Purdy, **Feelbad Britain** in P.Devine, A.Pearmain & D.Purdy (eds), **Feelbad Britain**, Lawrence & Wishart, London, 2009, ISBN 9781905007936. Also at www.hegemonics.co.uk

*are only two questions in politics: What should we do? And what shall we do? What we are saying is that, while there are undoubtedly tensions between "should" and "shall", between morality and practice, between visions and realities, they all need to be considered together if we are to begin making a political difference...*

*The democratic left seeks to combine the characteristic socialist belief in social equality and human solidarity with the civic republican ideals of positive freedom and democratic self-government and the green commitment to sustainable development and post-materialism. Do these values cohere? Could a society embodying them exist? Or is it a chimera? Two issues need to be distinguished here. One is whether a society with the requisite features would be able to cope with perennial problems facing all human societies — such as how to handle conflicting claims on available resources — and thus maintain itself as a going concern. The other, more obviously political, issue is whether such a society can be brought into being, starting from where we are now and taking into account probable barriers and sources of resistance...*

*How can we decide whether some imaginary social order could exist?... There are obvious tensions — between what is ideal and what is realistic, between grand aims and fine detail, between what needs to be sketched out now and what can be left for later elaboration, between defending what has already been achieved and fighting for something better. The important thing is to keep on exploring ideas for 'living otherwise', deliberately blurring the line between the way things are and the way they could be without confusing possible worlds with the realms of fantasy.*

*There is, however, a difference between visualising possible worlds and pursuing political projects. In politics, we have to reckon with constraints and pressures that can – indeed must – be set aside when articulating visions: institutional inertia, cultural habits, structural bias and political resistance, including the complex games that ensue when political agents try to anticipate the moves and counter-moves of their opponents. Thus, while values and visions are the stars we steer by, we still have to navigate in real time and space ...*

*It helps... if we distinguish between policies and projects. Policies are not just practical responses to perceived social problems: they are also political acts that impinge on the prevailing balance of forces. Hence, correctly judged, they are instruments for changing the political landscape, building new institutions and securing vantage-points for further advance. But timing is crucial. Policies need to be tailored to specific situations and adapted, dropped or picked up again as the situation changes, normally within an electoral timeframe. A project, by contrast, is a long-term undertaking informed by deep and lasting values. It should make sense of the past, identify the main problems facing society in the present and propose a strategy for tackling them in the future, including general principles and guidelines for producing policies (a policy paradigm).*

All this would constitute a left political culture.

There has often been scepticism as to whether such a culture was ever possessed by the British left. Tawney in his assertion that the Labour Party lacked a creed was essentially voicing such doubts, a feeling buttressed by the resolute hostility of the British left towards any kind of theorising. Inside the British Communist Party, for example, it was traditional to greet any such effort by insisting on "The concrete analysis of concrete situations, comrade" rather as though British society was one large building site. However, up until the 1980s, it was possible to see a fairly consistent left political culture even if one that was spread over a wide spectrum. Indeed, the existence of this culture, one capable of incorporating a wide range of apparently incompatible political views, was a major factor in sustaining the hegemonic position of the Labour Party in the British left.

David Marquand in his race through twentieth-century British politics calls it democratic collectivism[87] and he captures much of its essence; a belief that the objective of left political action consisted largely of a planned and ordered society based upon economic equality. What he fails to capture, however, is what Drucker called the 'ethos' of the movement, a surprising though perhaps understandable omission, from a founder member of the Social Democratic Party in 1981,

---

[87] D.Marquand, Britain Since 1918, Weidenfeld & Nicholson, London, 2008, ISBN 978-0-7538-2606-5. In particular pp. 60-67

the split which effectively initiated the events which destroyed this culture and which played a large part in the failure to develop any alternative.

Drucker defined ethos as including *"the traditions, beliefs, characteristic procedures and feelings which help to animate the members of the party"*. He was specifically referring to the Labour Party but with minor differences in emphasis his analysis could be extended across most of the left. This is not surprising given that, as McKibbin noted, the dominant code within the party was *"a trade-union code of behaviour"*, something endorsed by Drucker, which also encompassed most other areas of the left. This code defines what is now commonly referred to as the 'tribalism' of the LP, that is adherence to the movement rather than to any point of doctrinal principle. Writing in 1985 at the very moment when this culture was falling apart, Raphael Samuel lamented its passing, blaming the collapse on the *"radical individualism and the progressivism of the 1960s which made personal identity and individual self-assertion the highest good"*[88]. He went on to link this to a perceived failure at the heart of the trade-union code; *"Once the decision to strike becomes a matter of personal decision rather than of obedience to collective discipline, or of upholding **collective honour**, it is subject to all those discriminations and cross-currents which make it so difficult to cope with the everyday"* (my emphasis). Although a rather odd phrase, Samuel was right in pointing to a 'collective honour', as

---

[88] R.Samuel, *The Lost World of British Communism*, **New Left Review**, 154, 1985, p. 7

lying at the heart of left political culture of the time.

In 1979, Drucker believed that this ideology had to change though he was far to sanguine about the ease of transition.

> *Britain is moving from parliamentary democracy to corporate democracy ... In these new circumstances it may be more important to know which powerful interest-groups are united with which political parties than to know which party has won most votes or holds the most seats in the House of Commons. Labour is the immediate beneficiary of this change. My impression is that it will adjust its ideology to this new world more easily than will the Conservative Party...Labour's ideology is based upon the two-party electoral system. The basis of manifestoism is that the Labour Party will from time to time form a government of its own unaided by any other party after a general election victory. It presumes that the party leaders will not have to trade policies with the leaders of other parties in order to form coalition governments; and it presumes that these leaders will not have to, in effect, form coalitions with extra-parliamentary pressure-groups to carry out the party's will as government. Both these assumptions are now exposed as inadequate, for the two-party system is faltering.*[89]

Drucker could not have been more wrong about the direction British politics after 1979, though he was

---

[89] Drucker, p.116

hardly alone, but his strategic vision was correct. His perception of a faltering system was a 72.8% electoral turnout with thirty-nine MPs from minority parties. He would have been astonished to find the same system hobbling along with a turnout of 64% and treble the number of minority MPs. He was right that the left 'ethos' about which he wrote so perceptively would change; he could not have been expected to realise that it would be destroyed so quickly and that a bastardised form would carry on to sustain a right-wing Labour government in power for fully thirteen years after an interregnum lasting eighteen years.

This is the heart of the matter. New Labour actively participated in the final obliteration of the culture which had sustained not just the LP but the entire left for a hundred years but retained its skeleton as useful adjunct to support its relentless centralisation and control of the party. That this skeleton is now commonly called Labour 'tribalism' is a marker for just how debased a once complex and coherent culture has become.

There are signs that some people both inside and outside the LP are aware of this gaping hole and the need to find a new culture. The talk about 'finding new narratives', 'going back to core values' and 'renewing Labour' is really just such a search. An extended, if vacuous, example is provided by James Purnell in his explication of the Open Left project in the Demos think tank.[90] The fact that this is entitled *Renewing the Best of Labour Traditions* is all that one really needs to say

---

[90] James Purnell, Renewing the Best of Labour Traditions, http://www.openleft.co.uk/2010/01/10/renewing-the-best-of-labour-traditions/

about the ambition of this project. However, the fact that it is happening at all is a sign that the change foreseen thirty years ago by Drucker is, perhaps, now underway. However, the extraordinary hostility shown by some of Labour's elders to the tentative and probably unattainable suggestion of a 'progressive alliance' formed by a coalition of the Labour, the LibDems and the nationalists shows that the old tradition is still far from dead inside the party.

## Finding a New Culture

A political culture involves three, closely linked components; an over-arching social objective, a set of policies fitting the immediate social context and aimed at achieving this objective and some kind of agency, a political organisation able to mobilise support for these.

One of the achievements of the wider left in the past decade has been the slow emergence of the first of these, a project to supplant the collectivist aim of a planned economy structured around maximising economic growth with a sustainable economy based around principles of fairness and equality and of tackling the environmental crisis overtaking the world. It is not intended to spend any time here on detailing this project; there are several easily accessible sources.[91] It is possible to argue that it falls under the rubric of a general kind of 'socialism' but names are largely irrelevant.

However it is also a project which, despite much lip-service, is still resisted in many parts of the left,

---

[91] See, for example, C.Lucas and J.Porritt in **After the Crash: Reinventing the Left**, Lawrence and Wishart ebook, London 2010 and M.Prior, **Beyond Feelbad Britain**, *ibid*

where the idea that growth in the GNP remains the cornerstone of left policy still holds court. Porritt describes how *"The launch of our Prosperity without Growth? Report... in the run-up to the G20 Summit in 2009 reduced Treasury officials and advisors in Number 10 to apoplectic incredulity. 'Do you really not see that getting back to as high a level of economic growth as possible, just as fast as possible, is all that matters to this government?'* This kind of attitude remains embedded in the trade unions leading to potentially disastrous splits over issues such as the third runway at Heathrow and a new set of nuclear power stations.

However, despite this resistance, a reasonably well-defined over-arching objective for the left can be seen emerging from the ideological wreckage of the last decades of the twentieth century.

The same is true of a set of policies which could lead towards this objective. A general statement of these would be that the left encompasses those who believe in some measure:

- that social and collective responses to general social and economic issues are usually to be preferred to individual ones;

- that, in particular, market processes are undesirable and ineffective in providing public services;

- that these public services include education, health, public security as well as some other areas which might include some natural utility and transport monopolies and some aspects of housing;

169

- that environmental concerns, in particular global warming, require urgent and radical policy responses based upon social action rather than individual market-based options;

- that services such as health and education should be free to all without discrimination;

- that a practical and functioning democracy should exist in all areas of social activity including economic;

- that forms of ownership other than private may be preferred in many sectors of the economy;

- that all citizens are entitled to receive a basic level of financial support from the state if they are without personal resources;

- and that equality is a public good in its own right.

There is plenty of scope for the argument and dispute traditional on the left over these and they could be expanded, particularly internationally, but they encompass what most would think of as forming the broad left.

Clearly, this left is wider than what, historically, was called the socialist left whose core belief was that society operated under a general social and economic system called capitalism which could and should be replaced by an alternative system called socialism, systems which in both cases were essentially defined by ownership. It needs to be recognised that a significant part of the left, as defined above, is resistant to the very idea of over-arching systems and does not recognise any neat dichotomy into capitalist and socialist.

It also needs emphasising that much of the left now lives inside political areas which are by no means 'owned' by the left. Nationalism, the environment, the peace movement, a whole range of international issues such as resistance to Israeli oppression of Palestinians or the crisis in Darfur as well as dozens of local and regional initiatives have left participation but are not wholly of the left or fully defined by it. The environmental movement is a key example. Although the left has a prominent role in the Green Party, it is by no means the only grouping there whilst such as Zac Goldsmith have perfectly sustainable environmental credentials whilst being, politically, on the right.

Just how many people could be assembled under these headings is impossible to know; a personal guess would be around a hundred thousand activists with the majority being unaffiliated to any organised left group. In electoral terms, a left platform based upon the above principles might, at the moment, be able to get ten to fifteen per cent of votes cast. But numbers are, for now, largely irrelevant. The task faced on the left is how to fashion some kind of network from these disparate groups which can acknowledge each other and engage in debate about political strategy without attempting to denigrate the choices that have led to individual places of residence and with the objective of developing some discernible impact on practical politics.

This is not a new project. It can be seen forty years ago in the May Day Manifesto group and thirty years ago in Rowbotham, Segal and Wainwright imagining how the left might move *Beyond the Fragments*[92] and Prior and Purdy suggesting that the left should move *Out of the Ghetto*.[93] There were efforts in the 1990s to form some kind of red-green alliance which effectively amounted to a new kind of left unity. All failed though not without some initial success. Why should any new endeavour succeed now?

The negative answer to this is that there is really no alternative. Two efforts to work through the LP — one based upon a democratic left turn at the end of the 1970s, one on the New Labour centralised, pragmatic approach — have failed whilst the left outside the LP has fragmented in all directions without any clear purpose. The positive answer has to be that Britain is approaching a general political conjuncture which, as the previous analysis argues, is unstable and likely to give rise to seismic movement as the great colliding tectonic plates of Labour and Conservative, moving over each other, finally give rise to sudden shifts.

The left has no obvious path through the current political maze, the difficulty being that although words like 'coalition' and 'unity' are in vogue on the left, it is far from clear that there is any agreement on what they mean. When Jon Trickett wrote in October, 2007

> *We need to learn to multi task again; simultaneously reconnecting with all parts of the coalition into a new historic block. This is*

---

[92] S.Rowbotham, L.Segal and H.Wainwright, **Beyond the Fragments: Feminism and the Making of Socialism**, London, Merlin, 1979
[93] M. Prior and D. Purdy, *ibid*

*the task which Gordon Brown must address if he is to win. The first hundred days were devoted to emphasising the change of PM and also to establishing am impression of competence and strength. These are necessary attributes of governance but as the polls now show they do not amount to a strategy for reconnecting with Labour's missing millions. The stakes are high but the prize is a great one. Brown has the opportunity to create a coalition, win a fourth term and in the process change Britain into the social democratic country which is waiting to be born.[94]*

before disappearing into the Brown government, he failed to provide any details as to who exactly he envisaged as the membership of this coalition or indeed what it encompassed. The old New Labour electoral block? Bits of the LP? Or a wider political coalition? The key to understanding the ambiguity lies in the formative basis of the LP as a federal body which never progressed beyond this uneasy half-way house to become a genuine mass political party. For men like Trickett, the LP *was* a coalition of a wide range of social groups; for him the task of assembling a new historic block is essentially one of reassembling such a coalition inside the old formation. He still sees this as *the* coalition rather than envisaging *a* coalition.

In nearly all left groups, inside and outside the LP, there is also a lack of any clear political strategy apart from the nationalist parties in Scotland and Wales whose political target is clear; to blow away the Labour Party in their countries. The Green

---

[94] http://www.compassonline.org.uk/news/item.asp?n=940

Party still clings to a kind of slow-motion electoralism gradually building up a council base whilst having hopes of snatching a couple of parliamentary seats. The result in Brighton Pavilion which has given it a single MP is heartening but has to be recognised as something of an electoral freak, a constituency which is almost a four-way marginal allowing Caroline Lucas to be elected with 31% of the vote, the lowest in the country. On the extreme left, there is always talk of some kind of unity which then is blown away on rifts based upon arcane disputes often based on ancient history and, in any case, is based upon a definition of the 'left' which excludes any but residual Marxist-Leninists.

In Britain, there are only two past models for left unity. In the 1930s, popular fronts were assembled throughout Europe essentially based around opposition to some very real fascist threats and resting upon partial reassembly of previous splits between socialist parties into Communist and Social Democratic fractions, a split which largely passed Britain by. A more recent phase was the 1970s when most of the left essentially grouped, though in diverse ways, around a project base upon an alliance between Labour members and left unions to achieve a transformation of the LP, a project which was momentarily successful but which fell apart over internal dissension and a recovery of Labour's union base by the right. This kind of political path is now closed. Not only is Labour membership now much depleted and the unions essentially de-politicised, whilst retaining a crucial but basically bureaucratic role inside the party, but centralised control over the party machine is now effectively complete and beyond any democratic mobilisation.

The complexity of the problem is that unity needs to progress in two dimensions; bringing together both a semi-organised 'vertical left' and providing at least a bridge between this left and the 'horizontal left' with its disdain for electoral politics and its dislike of hierarchical organisation.

Inside the Labour, there were signs even before the election that some were starting to work on the reformation of the left after an expected Labour defeat. These include the unlikely double-act of Jon Cruddas and James Purnell, one having the Compass think-tank as his PR machine, the latter working out of a rather weird project in the Demos think-tank[95] which seeks to answer the question: What does it mean to be on the Left today? Both write freely about the 'left', without making much effort to define what they mean by this carpetbag word, and appear to be setting themselves up as Labour's pathfinders for its post-2010 world. One can expect much in the way of a 'narrative' involving 'paths to equality and individual empowerment' as well as ways to 'reclaim Labour's lost constituency' before the year is out.

The problem with both Cruddas and Purnell is that they appear to see the left as an inchoate mass just waiting to be mobilised for Labour if only the right policy buttons can be pressed. They lack any apparent sense of the current structure of the left; political life is frozen for them perpetually in 1997 when, as Blair children, (both have been Blair aides), they saw what seemed to be a united

[95] www.openleft.co.uk

coalition of the left supporting Labour. Both seem to regard the early Blair as their exemplar, promising a new world without being too specific about the details and gathering around them a joyous mass of the left.

Meanwhile, on the lonely extremities of the Labour Party, there did seem, before the election, to be the first stirrings of revolt. John McDonnell, perpetual leadership contender if he could only raise enough MP votes to be nominated, suggested standing as *"Labour MPs making it clear at the next election that they stand on a policy platform of real change as 'change candidates'"*[96]. It remains uncertain as to just what this meant. If mouthing off about the deficiencies of the leadership, then there's little new. If he meant standing with a published manifesto different to that prepared by the central machine then this would have meant mean deselection and expulsion. In the event, nothing of the kind happened and the few LRC MPs stood on the centrally-agreed platform.

This encapsulates the central contradiction of the Labour Representation Committee which McDonnell leads and of its largely Labour membership. Whilst fulminating against the policies of New Labour, they cannot take political positions which might either endanger their membership nor can they consider any real alliance with any part of the left outside the LP. They were vehement in their denunciation of any possible coalition with the LibDems and now can only call

---

[96] http://l-r-c.org.uk/press/labour-left-threatens-candidates-for-change-slate-if-policies-dont-change

for a "coalition against cuts" which appears to involve joining the LP.[97]

The problem is that neither of the two past models for left unity or coalition offer very much today. The anti-fascist common front of the 1930s was directed very narrowly and had very little by way of any internally-generated political culture. The role of the Labour Party as coalition is doomed beyond recall with the grip of a centralised, metropolitan machine if anything increasing. The general position appears to be to elect a new young (white male) leader who will express profound thoughts about the need for change and the revival of the party (sub-text: I am not Gordon Brown) and wait for the coalition to collapse and a general election which will bring Labour back to power once the incubus of Brown has been dropped. Business as usual with the brief flirtation with coalition forgotten

The obvious flaw with this approach is that the Tory/LibDem coalition may prove a good deal more stable than was immediately predicted. The dreadful record of Labour on a range of issues including human rights and civil liberties, the Afghan war and action on the banking system means that it is all too easy to put forward a number of measures which will be welcomed by the uneasy leftwing of the LibDems whilst Cameron would probably welcome the opposition, even defection, of some of his loonier right-wing MPs. Meanwhile overtures have already started to lure over a few Labour defectors, possibly more

---

[97] http://l-r-c.org.uk/press/the-left-will-not-support-a-cuts-coalition/

177

than a few. The public expenditure cuts will be large and create havoc in public services. But there main impact will be in the north of England and Scotland, Labour heartlands which can be written out of the electoral equation particularly after the constituency reduction and redistribution which is coming to eliminate (quite fairly) the 5% electoral bias held by Labour in May,

Whether it has been by fortune or design, Cameron and Clegg may have stumbled on something of a dream (or nightmare, depending on ones viewpoint) scenario, the creation of a new political bloc stretching from slightly to the left of the centre to the right, a bloc which was always just out of reach of Labour however hard they tried. Such a bloc would be strengthened by the introduction of the alternative vote electoral system and could cope with the floating away of the Celtic nations. This latter development would prove the ultimate dream ticket for Cameron as without Scotland and Wales, Labour has very little hope of winning in England.

This may or may not happen. But over the next two or three years the British left has its own problems which need urgent solution for unless consumed by a much greater fire than seems likely, the old hulk will still sail on though without much rigging and with a mutinous crew. It will still a have formidable electoral machine, union finance and can rely, to a degree, on its old saviour — solidarity. The wider left will have to consider its options carefully in developing some kind of joint action on an agreed programme of reform and general policy principles such as listed above to enable the left to emerge as a significant force in national politics.

Left Out: Policies for a Left Opposition

This is the perfect political storm combining economic recession with a crisis of legitimacy of the entire political system and, specifically, of the political vehicle which has for over a hundred years carried the aspirations of the British left. If nothing but business as usual emerges from this storm then the left will miss an historic chance to form a genuine left formation in British politics.

# Left Out: Policies for a Left Opposition

# SOCIAL DEMOCRACY IN PERSPECTIVE

## Willie Thompson

### *The Background*

It was with startled surprise that I realised earlier this year that the UK (or at least the English part of it) has by now been under Thatcherite and quasi-Thatcherite rule nearly as long as it was under the post-1945 social democratic settlement (which Conservative governments of the day never seriously interfered with) – thirty-one years in the one case, thirty-four in the other.

By the standards of European social democracy the British variant was somewhat anomalous. Like the others it was the creation of a labour movement with industrial workers at its core, like them, as Eric Hobsbawm notes,[98] it had to transform itself into a national cross-class political force rather than a sectional one in order to attain governmental office both at national and widespread local levels.

The difference was that organised British labour had been integrated into the pre-existing political structure decades before the formation of the Labour Party, 1900-1906. At first it did not even have a political programme (or acquire one until 1918). Its only objective was to gain parliamentary representation. In the opening words of Ralph Miliband's *Parliamentary Socialism*, *"Of all*

---

[98]Eric Hobsbawm, 'World Distempers' *New Left Review* 61 (Second series) Jan/Feb 2010, pp.133-52

*political parties claiming socialism to be their aim, the Labour Party has always been one of the most dogmatic – not about socialism but about the parliamentary system"*. It had absorbed deep into its culture the values of Victorian liberalism, and a large component of its membership only abandoned with extreme reluctance their previous allegiance to the Liberal Party. Trade unions might include pictures of Marx on their banners and syndicalism make serious progress among some of their rank and file, but among their leadership and in the political sphere neither of these had a look-in.

By contrast, social democracy on the continent was on the whole inclined towards a Marxist understanding of class relations and some of the parties had a specific Marxist ancestry, especially the SPD, the German flagship of the Socialist International established in 1889. The First World War transformed the outlook of nearly all, and social democracy, as it was to be known in the twentieth century, emerged out of the crucible of that conflict. The ostensible revolutionism of their formal politics was confronted with the realities of 1914, when, reneging on pre-war commitments, they aligned themselves with 'the nation' as defined by the respective ruling elites (also accepted, it has to be said, by the great majority of their members) and assisted 'their' governments in prosecuting the mutual slaughter – or even joined them.

Another existential crisis confronted these parties in 1917 and its aftermath, with the Russian Revolution, the establishment of the Bolshevik regime and the formation two years later of the

Communist International. Here was a party in power, a regime allegedly based on workers' power, claiming to be the only real Marxists, recognising the total bankruptcy of all bourgeois institutions, intent on the total transformation social relations along with the expropriation of the propertied classes – and eager to spread its form of revolution around the world. The social democrat leaders for the most part, once they understood its intentions turned from it with horror. The SPD leader Friedrich Ebert, proclaimed on the morrow of the 1918 German revolution which lifted him into power,

> *First, we do not intend to confiscate any bank or savings bank deposits nor any sums in cash or banknotes or other valuable papers deposited in the bank safes... Therefore, we address to the employers the urgent appeal to help with all their strength the restoration of production ...*

This sort of approach became the theme of all the social democratic parties, and so far as the UK was concerned it was already the reality in any case. It did not exclude public ownership of certain economic assets (the European railways were publicly owned already under impeccably bourgeois regimes) but it certainly did exclude any fundamental challenge to the existing power elites.

The characteristics of social democracy were rigid constitutionalism, even in constitutions like the British which were flagrantly only semi-democratic, The rules of law were to be strictly observed and no project undertaken to 'expropriate the expropriators', to use the Marxist terminology. In the UK the Labour Party leaders even came to reverence feudal hangovers in the state and the absurd ritualism around parliament and government. The state was treated by them as a national institution, never seen as primarily an instrument of class rule. For them politics was a gentlemanly dialogue, not 'civil war by other means', as Miliband adapts Clausewitz's famous aphorism.

Britain was the only country in Europe where its social democratic party did not split between reformists who maintained the traditions and the name, and communists attaching themselves to the Third International. In Britain the infant Communist Party had to be formed instead out of minor left wing groupings outside the Labour Party.

In effect, like its counterparts elsewhere, the Labour Party came to form the left wing of social liberalism. None of these parties, including the British, was of course a homogenous entity, but comprised within themselves diverse trends along a right-left spectrum, with the left having decidedly less respect for the powers and the institutions that be. However invariably they were controlled by their more cautious and conservative elements, always determined to remain within constitutional limits and appease the power elites – even in the unusually radical Swedish instance.

In Britain this was particularly marked, not least because – and in this the UK differed – the trade unions were an integral part of the party; in fact they had established it. Not unnaturally, trade unions sought stability as a primary aim, not merely to protect their very considerable material assets, but because it was crucial to their members' life chances. Upheaval in the state meant probable breakdown in the economy; impoverishment, likely destitution, even possible imprisonment or death if a really reactionary regime took advantage of the disturbance to impose itself.

It is not therefore necessarily a criticism of the social democratic parties that they adopted the political postures described above. It could certainly be argued that nothing else was practicably feasible in the circumstances of the time. Nevertheless, as Aneurin Bevan once remarked, that as he got nearer to what he had thought to be the sources of power – from local government to Parliament, to the cabinet – real power always seemed to be somewhere else, as indeed it was: in the civil service, the military, the police, the judiciary, the secret services; the enforcement agencies of the state and the propertied elements on whose behalf they did the enforcing.

In circumstances of world economic depression social democracy could hope to achieve very little. The Swedish exception of the 1930s was favoured by unique conditions –small population, a wealth of natural resources – and the demand for raw materials created by German rearmament. In conditions of global economic expansion however, underpinned by American power and cheap oil, such as prevailed in the fifties and sixties, there was much greater scope. The Attlee government of 1945-50, even earlier, had some undoubtedly remarkable achievements (even it they were oversold), but these were made possible only by the consumer austerity which ultimately undid his administration, the dollars supplied by Marshall Aid, and consequent vassalage to the US.

Eric Hobsbawm has commented that the two decades after 1950 (ironically, Labour was out of office during most of them) were the probably the ones which came nearest to realising the vision of the British socialist pioneers. Until the end of the fifties some of the European social democrat parties had retained a platonic formal attachment to their Marxist heritage, but by the turn of that decade found it safe and convenient to abandon, as the SPD did in 1959 at their Bad Godesberg conference.

The accomplishment was acclaimed immoderately in Anthony Crosland's 1956 *The Future of Socialism*, where he argued that a combination of responsibly-used trade union strength, newly-discovered social responsibility on the part of business, together with Keynesian demand and monetary management by governments, had eliminated the danger of economic breakdown and secured stability and growth for all time to come. Therefore – and this was a central contention of his argument – the legal ownership of productive and service facilities was an irrelevant consideration. Donald Sassoon in *One Hundred Years of Socialism* noted that this outlook, *"was shared by all socialist revisionists throughout Europe in the 1950s and was a necessary part of their new vision"*.[99] A very similar vision for the USA was propagated by Daniel Bell in *The End of Ideology*, in 1960. Bell and Crosland were good friends and

---

[99] Donald Sassoon, *One Hundred Years of Socialism*, I B Tauris, 1996, p.245

both connected with the Congress for Cultural Freedom, a CIA front.

## The sixties and seventies

In the course of the next decade however, the gilt was beginning to come off the capitalist economic miracle and signs of problems to multiply. Firstly intensified international competition with the industrial recovery of Germany and Japan and other European countries as well, which was to destroy the British motor vehicle industry, beginning with motor-cycles, then cars and finally industrial vehicles; shipbuilding; locomotive manufacture; electronics. In the UK by the mid-sixties the deindustrialisation process was well underway.

Secondly the mountain of debt built up by US administrations as a result particularly of the Vietnam war but also through its overall military expenditure, which by the end of the decade undermined the position of the dollar as a world financial stabiliser. Most importantly of all however, as Andrew Glyn and Bob Sutcliffe demonstrated in the British case, the combination of full employment with strong trade union movements shifted the balance between labour and capital so that profit rates were steadily eroded. The symptom of this development was accelerating inflationary trends. The oil price hike which followed the Yom Kippur war of 1973 tipped an increasing unstable global economy over into the long-term recession from which it had, even before the banking crash of 2008, never properly emerged.

For a number of reasons the post-war British economy was historically weak, especially on account of its emphasis on capital export and on military commitments far beyond its strength as a result of on its rulers' insisting on the pretence, which its social democracy accepted without question, to be a great power.[100]

Harold Wilson's governments of 1964-70 felt the force of these realities. His administration, especially after a convincing electoral victory in 1966, entered office with ambitious plans for technological and managerial restructuring of the economy; plans which had to be abandoned almost as soon as they were printed. The 1966-70 government was plagued with balance of payments crises and endured, in the days of fixed exchange rates, forced devaluation of sterling in 1967. Popular approval was squandered by its unquestioning political and diplomatic deference to the US during the Vietnam war – the economic crisis ensured that it did not dare to do otherwise, though at least Wilson had the sense not to commit British troops. As an earnest of things to come, for the first time in the history of Labour governments or indeed the Labour Party, its leadership provoked direct conflict with the trade union movement; the issue being Wilson's attempt to impose compulsory wage restraint. This social democratic government's record was one of dismal failure everywhere, except in the one area of civil and social liberties – and that was under the management of a Home Secretary who was a Liberal in everything but name.

---

[100] However it should be kept in mind that the armaments manufactured by BAE are the UK's principal material export.

Thus even before the end of the post-war boom, as economic strains intensified, the hitherto tight unity of British social democracy and British labourism was starting to unravel. With it went the broader, largely hidden corporatism, examined in detail by Keith Middlemas, between capital, organised labour and governments of whichever colour, which had characterised the decades since the late twenties (if not since the early century). Central to the particular ideology of labourism was the principle of 'free collective bargaining', an institution and practice coming at that point under increasing attack from all sides.

## *'Interesting times'*

The interwar economic crisis brought harsh and bitter times for European social democracy; the post-1973 crisis proved to be its nemesis (and that of the US New Deal liberalism which was its equivalent). There was a very important difference, ideological rather than material, between the two eras – social democracy could not be blamed for the interwar crisis, and where it survived persecution, could present itself convincingly as the remedy. After 1973 the post-war settlement on social democratic principles could be, and was, presented as the source of the problem. Wages were too high, likewise social expenditure. Labour was too strong, investment opportunities were blocked by public ownership and regulation, Keynesian demand management generated inflation – hence investment dropped off, markets seized up and everybody was worse off. The recommended solution was the nostrums of nineteenth century *laissez-faire* economics adumbrated by such gurus as Friedreich von Hayek

189

– which had the fortunate quality of fitting in exactly with the ambitions of some very powerful vested interests.

From the early seventies an intense and well-financed campaign was undertaken, both ideologically and in policy terms to reverse, the social democratic or quasi-social democratic consensus that had characterised the previous decades. Every West European state was affected, including latecomers to social democrat administration such as Portugal, Spain and Greece, and so was the United States. Right-wing think-tanks proliferated, as did powerful media outlets popularising their message; social democratic administrations found their projects blocked and frustrated and their finances bankrupted

Neither social democracy not labour movements surrendered without a struggle, and this was particularly marked in the UK. In the  late sixties the trade unions successfully blocked Wilson's attempt to impose government wage controls. His successor, Edward Heath, a Conservative, but still essentially attached to the post-war consensus, tried again, but in 1971 was compelled to back down over plant closures by the UCS work-in and the popular support it evoked in Scotland; was humiliated by the TUC when he tried to meet defiance of his Industrial Relations Act by imprisoning some dockers, in 1972 was defeated again by the miners over wage controls and finally in 1974 overthrown by them (and the electorate).

The character of British social democracy was profoundly affected by these events, which set it on the course that was ultimately to lead to New Labour. The failures of the 1960s Wilson governments and the character of Heath's resulted in the adoption by the Labour Party conference in 1973 of what came to be known two years later as 'The Alternative Economic Strategy', which specified reflation, public ownership planning price controls, industrial democracy and import restrictions. It amounted to a decent social democratic programme; its weakness was that it could have only have been implemented in a siege economy which would have greatly impaired consumer satisfaction and would have been relentlessly assaulted by both national and international capital along with all their political and ideological apparatuses.

The 'Social Contract' negotiated between the British trade unions and the unstable Labour governments which followed Heath's defeat was only a shadow of the AES, but even so probably the best that was possible in the circumstances. In effect the trade unions agreed to *voluntary* curbs on wage rises in return for promises of income redistribution, extended public ownership and enhancement of the 'social wage' – that is welfare amenities.

There remains in circulation a persistent myth that the trade unions reneged on the Social Contract, were responsible for the 'Winter of Discontent' of 1978-9 and opened the door to Thatcherism. In reality the exact opposite is nearer the case. It was the government which reneged, not the unions – especially in the Healy budget of 1976, which, in response to the conditions of an IMF loan to address the current balance of payments crisis, ditched every one of the commitments made in 1974. The union leaders nevertheless made every effort, in spite of all the traditions of free collective bargaining, to restrain their membership – who were suffering real income reductions and seeing no improvement in the social wage – from taking industrial action to redress their grievances, and largely succeeding until 1978, when the dam finally broke.

At the same time, in the political dimension of British social democracy, very significant changes were occurring. In 1975 Stuart Holland published *The Socialist Challenge*, which, in addition, to the principles embodied in the Alternative Economic Strategy, advocated state holdings in key enterprises and planning compulsory agreements between business and government, an expansion of the arguments he had deployed when he participated in the drafting of the Wilson's government's Industry Act of that year. The act as it emerged however, completely neutered these proposals, as it specified that its measures would be 'voluntary', in other words, inoperative.

The chain of disillusionments suffered under these Wilson/Callaghan governments, which gave every indication of repeating the experience of the 1960s Labour administrations in an even less favourable economic environment, provoked a revolt by activists at the base of the Labour Party, which, combined with a more effective strategy, better organisation, the demoralisation of the right and the indignation of rank-and-file trade unionists, gained success in a manner which no previous left-wing attempt had ever done.

They succeeded not only in winning majorities at the Party Conference, once again, for example, including nuclear disarmament among the Party objectives, but more importantly in altering the Party's constitution to make it more responsive to rank-and-file pressures, taking away the exclusive power of MPs to elect the Party's leader and constituency organisations more control over the selection of these MPs. The objective was to secure a parliamentary Labour Party which, with an electoral majority, would seriously challenge the entrenched power of capital and the capitalist state. For this reason the trend was welcomed by the non-social democratic parts of the left, from the Communist Party to the Trotskyist and neo-Trotskyist sects; the latter, evading Labour Party proscription of their membership, actually participated in the process, especially the Revolutionary Socialist League, aka the Militant group. These in 1983 secured control of Liverpool city council, while two years earlier Ken Livingstone, another left-winger, though not a Militant, had become leader of the Greater London Council. In the Parliamentary Labour Party the former left-wing firebrand Michael Foot was elected leader, following Callaghan's electoral defeat and resignation, defeating in the process the right-wing Denis Healey.

## The early eighties

The developments of the late seventies and early eighties understandably produced panic among the British establishment, and no less the traditionalist Labour Party right-wing. It looked for a time as though British social democracy might become something more like what the name had originally signified. Indeed in 1981 a faction of the party's alarmist right wing broke away to form what they termed the Social Democratic Party, an impudent piece of identity theft.[101]

The individuals behind it were a mixed bunch. It is difficult to imagine Roy Jenkins OM PC as a revolutionary of any sort, yet in the sixties as Home Secretary he had presided over the British share in the last conquests of the bourgeois revolution, sweeping away a large portion of the socio-cultural garbage inherited from previous centuries such as judicial murder and a great deal of sexual obscurantism. David Owen, described by one source as a 'serial resigner', by contrast had nothing in the least progressive about him, in fact was a right-wing Tory with a Labour Party label who hungered for the days of British imperial power and despised the Labour Party opposition to the Suez adventure in 1956. A not very impressive collection of Labour Party careerists whose jobs and status in Westminster or local government were put at risk by the changes taking place, followed them into the SDP, as did a fair number of honest individuals who misguidedly imagined that this party represented something new and imaginative. The general attitude of the left who were now making the running in the Labour Party was to celebrate 'good riddance'.

Unfortunately for the left their hopes were as groundless as were the fears of their enemies. As Patrick Seyd expressed it, they made the error of mistaking their victories in the inner-party struggle for a reflection of what was happening in society as a whole. The British political culture is a very

---

[101] Another such was naming their think-tank after R H Tawney.

conservative one, whose atavistic responses were expertly played upon by the establishment media, especially the Murdoch press. The minuscule votes received by the Communist Party and the ultra-left organisations in general elections were an indication of the true state of affairs among the broader public. There was no possibility in these circumstances of a left-wing social democracy ever winning government office.

The left wing tide had peaked in the autumn of 1981, when at the annual Conference its representative, Tony Benn stood against Denis Healey for the Deputy Leadership of the Party, and lost by the narrowest of margins. His victory would probably have split the party irretrievably, but narrow defeat demoralised the left, and the organisations which had promoted its agenda either fell to pieces, moved to the right or slid into internal disputation. The exception was Militant, but that had now lost friends and credibility and was by stages excluded from the party.

The surviving, battered social-democratic Labour Party was unable to put together a convincing enough narrative to win electoral support and suffered appropriately in the 1983 general election, not least because the of the SDP defection, which for a time was able to tap into a current of frustration and political discredit for the Labour Party under Michael Foot's less-than-inspired leadership. The Liberal-SDP Alliance polled strongly and came very close to overtaking Labour and establishing itself as the official Opposition. The reservoir of traditional support which Labour still possessed combined with first-past-the-post electoral system to save the party from total debacle, but it was a near thing.

## 1983 to 1992

The Thatcher government now began seriously to implement its vision of post-welfare Britain, destroying the strength of trade unionism partly by restrictive legislation and total victory over the miners, but principally by laying waste the industries in which the powerful unions were based. Simultaneously it plundered the socially-owned assets which had underpinned the welfare system – gas, electricity, water, urban transport, municipal housing, and embarked upon a programme of social engineering to ensure that the workforce and the masses generally could never again threaten or challenge the superiority of their betters.

In face of this unprecedented assault British social democracy did what social democrats had become accustomed to doing – it capitulated. (To be fair, the same kind of thing was happening in other West European countries as well). The book by Richard Heffernan and Mike Marquese, *Defeat from the Jaws of Victory* gives an account of what happened from the point of view of the defeated left. The title is a little strange, since it is hard to imagine what jaws of victory were in the picture,[102] and the account is anything but balanced, giving little weight to the circumstances that the new Labour leadership of Kinnock and Hattersley were up against and the limitations of choice that they faced.

---

[102] Unless it refers to the expected Kinnock victory which never happened in the 1992 election.

Nevertheless it expounds very clearly the atmosphere of intrigue, manipulation, backstabbing and lack of principle which characterised the decade and the sinister role played, even then, by Peter Mandelson. Suffice to say that in the course of Kinnock's leadership every one of the radical political commitments that had been adopted by the party in the days of the left's ascendancy was ditched. The internal constitutional changes remained, but they proved to be as easily manipulable by the leadership as had been the earlier system. The trade-union leaders whose collective veto over the party's direction still applied, increasingly desperate under the Thatcherite cosh, were willing to back any party leadership which looked capable of restoring the party's electability, and endorsed the Kinnockite agenda. Moreover its path was smoothed by the fact that significant elements previously in the radical camp, the 'soft left', – Jack Straw, Charles Clarke, Dave Blunkett and Gordon Brown may be mentioned – had made their peace with the new regime and were to the forefront in promoting its project.

Once more British social democracy had returned to the stance from which it had only briefly emerged in the aftermath of the Second World War, subservience to capital complemented by total acceptance of the basic institutions of the British economy and state, promising change only at the margin. Even before Tony Blair took over the party was proposing to reverse scarcely any of the Thatcherite inflictions or to restore public control over what she and her successor had taken away. Devolution and the minimum wage were the

197

only significant courses on the menu with a social democratic flavour.

## *Social Democracy and the Communist Debacle*

All this (along with what was happening contemporaneously elsewhere in Europe) might appear all the more surprising in view of the total collapse of social democracy's great opponent on the left. Between 1989 and 1991 the Soviet bloc disintegrated and the Soviet Union followed it into oblivion, while the other great communist power. China, while remaining united and authoritarian, sprinted as fast as possible towards a capitalist economy[103] with a dragooned labour force. Communist parties not in power either fell apart, closed themselves down or totally changed their character.

It might have been anticipated that such developments would rebound to the benefit of social democracy, now that there was no longer any serious rival on the left, and indeed there were observers who expected that to happen, but nothing could have been further from the truth, for social democratic parties, least of all British Labour, did not launch an aggressive and vigorous vindication of themselves as holding to an alternative vision of socialism whose hour had now arrived. Instead they shrunk further into the political shadows, accepting with steadily greater certitude that there existed no conceivable alternative to globalised capitalism operating according to uncontrolled

---

[103] Though its government still keeps control over the 'commanding heights' such as the banking system.

market criteria. The very term 'socialism' was extruded more and more from their vocabularies and any occasional mention of it by a Labour leader would evoke something of a media flurry.

Therefore far from raising the profile of social democracy the communist collapse strengthened the conviction that unregulated capitalism was the only game in town, for the competing model, the command economy being the only one ever seriously advanced, had failed totally and comprehensively – and its discredit, amplified by every mainstream media outlet, spilled over onto other versions of socialism as well, from the mildest social democracy to Trotskyite revolutionism. The overthrown parties in the Soviet bloc survived perhaps better than might have been expected, but only at the cost of abandoning every Marxist pretension and embracing the capitalist reality. Moreover, with the disappearance of its enemy and rival pole of attraction, capital, represented particularly by the USA, felt far less need to conciliate its workforces either industrially or politically and so the ability of social democracy to win concession was correspondingly weakened.

## New Labour

Back in 1962 an aspirant to Labour candidature in a bye-election ruined his chances when at the selection conference he argued that one of his claims to the position was that he would look good on television. He was rejected amid ridicule. However when in 1994, when Tony Blair attained the Labour leadership, his principal qualification was indeed that he was media-savvy and his Mephistopheles, Peter Mandelson, an arch-manipulator of political communication, even more so. Blair was appointed because the party membership and the trade unions which sustained it were desperate after their long exclusion from office and Blair was believed to be a leader with the skills and a team competent enough to win the next election. His elevation, following the sudden death of John Smith, could be regarded as a historic accident, but ('cometh the time cometh the person') it was highly indicative of the direction in which British social democracy was heading. It was a perceptive *Guardian* reader who commented at that time in the letter columns that if this man ever became prime minister he would prove to be even worse than Thatcher.

In 1992 I predicted that the Labour Party would in due course become indistinguishable from the Liberals (or Liberal Democrats as they had by then taken to calling themselves) and also, ironically, that a Liberal-Labour coalition might be no bad thing as it could possibly pull the Labour Party a little more to the left. Blair lost no time in deleting from the party's constitution, and replacing with an anodyne substitute, the famous Clause 4 which stated as an aspiration the party's commitment to social ownership of the means of 'production, distribution and exchange', which had indeed summarised the essence of social democracy – I have to admit that I myself (at that point a Labour party member) voted to accept the deletion on the grounds that there was no point in having an aspiration without any possibility of ever being implemented by any foreseeable Labour administration, and dropping it would simply declare more emphatically the party's real character. The Tories were by then so unpopular anyway that probably it made very little difference, and the commentator in 1997 was no doubt accurate who noted that Labour would win even if Blair were to be discovered in a male brothel.

The rest, as they say, is history. Promises (even manifesto commitments) were violated, wars launched on the basis of flagrant lies, repressive legislation (modelled on the apartheid regime's) forced through on a scale not seen since the nineteenth century, refugees harassed and tormented, and what Tory governments had left in the public sector privatised or lined up for privatisation. When funding was allocated for any form of welfare or social amenity it was almost invariably accompanied with threats and intimidatory demands. Gordon Brown, the editor of the *Red Paper on Scotland* and biography of Jimmy Maxton[104], was as Chancellor even handing funding to the Adam Smith Institute to pursue privatisation schemes in the Third World, and as Prime Minister invited Margaret Thatcher herself to coffee and a friendly chat in Downing Street.

To be sure, Blair also led the Labour Party to another two decisive election victories, but that had more to do with the miserable quality of the opposition than any merit on the part of his administration. With developments in the Liberal Democrats after 2005 it became clear that there were no longer three major parties with opposing platforms but rather three rival factions of the Thatcherite party. It is only fair to note however, that this type of evolution was not specific to New Labour, but was occurring all over the world.

---

[104] Which he even had reissued when he was in office.

British New Labour was preceded by similar shifts in the governing Labour parties of Australia and New Zealand. It was accompanied by equivalents throughout Europe whilst, in the USA, Bill Clinton's presidency continued and extended the policies of Ronald Reagan's. Everywhere there took place a dramatic shift in wealth and power from lower income groups into the hands of the wealthy and super-wealthy – a process concealed from clear visibility by the encouragement among the former of massive indebtedness as a substitute for rising real incomes, a flock of vultures which came home to roost in 2008.

The conviction that seized New Labour, as it had done the previous Tory administrations, was that when it came to the economy in general or public services in particular, 'private good, public bad' – not the experience of anyone who gets on the wrong side of private companies or seeks redress for their inefficiencies. In every sphere, from transport through education to communications or water supply, privatisation has invariably meant a deterioration in the quality of service along with worsened conditions for their workforces.

In the editorial of January 2010 celebrating fifty years of the *New Left Review*, the editor Susan Watkins writes that the 1990s saw an international landscape that would have looked like sci-fi dystopia in 1960,

> *... the Kremlin's economic policy run by Friedmanites, the General Secretary of the CCP lauding the stock exchange; Yugoslavia, the most pluralist and successful of the workers' states decimated by IMF austerity purposes and subjected to a three-month*

> *NATO bombing campaign cheered on by liberal opinion in the West; social democratic parties competing to privatize national assets and abolish labour gains. Neo-liberalism reigned supreme, enshrining a model of unfettered capital flows and financial markets, deregulated labour and integrated production chains.*[105]

And it got worse.

Social democracy has been abandoned by social democrats, but, again, that should not be attributed simply to ill-will, though here has been plenty of that as well. A successful social democratic project requires two preconditions – firstly, a well-functioning capitalist economy so that resources can be diverted into social provision without injuring business too deeply, and in consequence class struggle is dampened. In other words, social democracy, is, to put it cruelly, parasitic upon capitalism. No social democratic government anywhere has ever tried to replace it with something different or even seriously contemplated doing so (Crosland tried to solve the dilemma simply by redefining capitalism). The second precondition is a strong, disciplined and self-confident labour movement capable of putting capital on the defensive and making it unwilling to try conclusions but to decide instead that its interests would be better served by negotiation. The two things are of course linked.

There is little reason to expect that either of these conditions will return, particularly the second,

---

[105] Susan Watkins, 'Shifting Sands', *New Left Review* 61 (new series) January-February 2010, p.5.

whether in the UK or elsewhere. Social democracy, it can be safely concluded, is a busted flush, incapable of developing any vision that could inspire large masses of followers. When voters vote for social democrat parties nowadays they do so only as the least worst option and with very few expectations. The possibility remains that an especially talented leader may evoke enthusiasm, such as Obama did in the USA, but once elected their limitations, or rather the limitations of the political structures, become plain, as has been the case with Obama.

## *'The by-product of a casino'*

An interesting article by John Lanchester in the *London Review of Books* earlier this year pointed out that regardless of the outcome of the election the result would be much the same. Either of the main parties, he wrote, or any combination of them was going to make the masses in Britain pay for the irresponsibility of the bankers and financial manipulators – which may of course then give an opening to really sinister forces. (Happily, in the eventual outcome these were crushed, but that may only be temporary – they haven't gone away). The difference from the present, he argued would be one of degree rather than kind regardless of who is the premier. We shall see, but what is absolutely clear is that the axe is going to be taken to what remains of the public services. 'Hard decisions' – hard for those who have them inflicted on them, not for those who make them, well protected by their income streams. 'Efficiency savings' – a pure Orwellism that invariably implies worse service and worse employment conditions, generating deadly scandals of all kinds, especially in social work and medicine.

A Tory election poster proclaimed "Let's cut benefits for those who refuse work offers". Nostalgia for the nineteenth-century deterrent workhouse has never been far from the consciousness of that political element. That poster however was tapping into a very widespread media-inflamed sentiment among voters (even those likely to fall victim to its proposal), as I discovered during discussions preceding the election. There exists an enormous public deficit to be plugged, somebody has to suffer, and the project to blame the most helpless sections of the public for the wreckage the financial manipulators have wrought has had an alarming degree of success. Less than a week after the election David Miliband, the first careerist to announce his candidacy for the Labour Party leadership, was implicitly lending his support to these prejudices and reaffirming that there could be no return to what Labour had previously claimed to stand for.

One might borrow a phrase to define the Labour Party of today – 'really-existing social-democracy'. Though losing the election the Labour Party survived it rather better than expected – which in spite of everything showed that there was still a reservoir of public feeling attached to the post-war settlement and perceived that the Tories represented the greater threat to what remains of it. Classic social democracy, in Britain and elsewhere has in the past certainly eased conditions of life for impoverished and vulnerable people and the members of the workforce, living from week to week or month to month on their wages, salaries or benefits. To do so, albeit not very substantially, it trimmed the claws and clipped the wings of capital, but that was made possible only by a generally expanding world economy with the capitalist industrialised nations as principal beneficiaries.

In view of the developments discussed above the New Labour leaders decided that if they ever reached office, while there might be constitutional or culture innovations (for example devolution and civil partnerships), no significant alterations would be made to the Thatcherised economy, except in a more Thatcherised direction. They assumed that with a little light-touch steering it would produce resources in abundance that could be used to fund any welfare measures that might be adopted, fund privatised public services, and still leave plenty over to provide for what Marx referred to as the 'Law and the Prophets of capital' – accumulation. In other words, the economy as a whole and social expenditure in particular  would continue to be dependent on what Keynes once described as the 'by-product of a casino'.

In the editorial article of *New Left Review* March/April 2010, Tony Wood dismisses the arguments that had been presented on the left for continuing to vote for that party, particularly the 'lesser evil' one; quotes a Labour supporter who asked, 'who would care if the Labour Party, politically and morally decrepit as it is, lost the next election'? and declares it to be unsalvageable – 'There is no reason why voters should be any more sentimental about the Labour Party than it has been about them'. He ends, 'Good riddance, this execrable government has to go' – as indeed it has done. One might disagree with his conclusion – *Labour Briefing* supported a Labour victory, not on the 'lesser evil' argument, but because a Tory one, 'would set back the conditions of struggle, possibly for many years' – but there is no doubting the strength and accuracy of Wood's analysis. A casual look at the three main party manifestos reinforces the point – if the party names weren't attached to them, it would be difficult to be certain which was which.

## *Thinking about tomorrow*

What then ought we to do? My own view is that the best option currently for the left is for its adherents to join the Green Party. This is a political movement with a great deal of enthusiasm, energy and commitment behind it and it has now shown itself to be electorally credible. Above all, its project is the most vitally essential one that exists today. Unless the present ruinous stampede to catastrophe is checked and reversed all other bets are off and the collapse of civilisation will be one of the more optimistic scenarios.

Joining the Green Party is no panacea of course, and that party is far from being at present a satisfactory vehicle for a socialist project. It is not, as has been pointed out by some green leftists, a socialist party. However, starting off as a purely environmentalist lobby, its positions have already become social democratic, and the logic of its programme is steadily carrying it in a socialist direction, a development which can only be accelerated by an influx of socialists. It is also protected from being absorbed by capitalism in the manner of social democracy by the fact that is standpoint is radically incompatible with capital's lifeblood – economic growth at any cost.

However, more is necessary. The starting point for that 'more' is the tricky question of what we actually mean by socialism. The concept itself is almost two centuries old, and if these decades have taught us anything it should be that socialism, however defined, is a very difficult enterprise indeed and that there are no easy answers. That, more than anything, is at the root of the sectionalism and sectarianism that have been the movement's worst affliction – worse, if anything, than the enmity of its opponents – and  have brought many a promising beginning to an unhappy end, most recently in the British context, the Scottish Socialist Party.

Strategies to overcome the power of the entrenched elites in control of exploitative societies with all the formidable apparatus of deceit and repression at their disposal, however seemingly impossible, are nevertheless the easier part. Reconciling high levels of material welfare with the environmental safeguards, social cohesion and personal freedoms which should accompany them is mind-bendingly complex and more challenging still. Nevertheless a vision of the future which incorporates these elements has to be developed, otherwise we will simply go round in circles until the environmental catastrophe overtakes us.

So far as our own political unit, the UK, which is all that we can work upon, is concerned, nothing less will suffice (with all the difficulty that implies) than a profound shift in the nature of the British political culture – though that proposition has to take into account that Britain is no longer a single unit and the political cultures in Scotland, Wales, Northern Ireland – and even different parts of England are seriously different. In Scotland (and Wales to a lesser extent) classic social democracy still dominates the public consciousness, though disputed between two bitterly antagonistic parties.

Existing bodies of defence and protest – from Liberty to the Stop the War Coalition, and parties with some credibility, such as the minor nationality parties or the Green Party are invaluable, but insufficient. A body with the specific project of establishing the framework for a viable socialism and shifting the political culture in that direction has great potential – if it could be realised. I am of course not unaware of the obstacles in the way of the formation and survival of such a coalition

It would be worth making the attempt – at any rate to see whether such a thing was possible – to establish a network using all the opportunities offered by the internet, to do two things. Firstly, to conduct sane and temperate discussions and interchange around the problems involved, aimed at developing a conceptual framework for what a feasible socialism might look like. Its initial aim would be to challenge the presumption of 'private good, public bad' and reassert the appropriateness of public ownership and control for public services and amenities, such as telecommunications, water, electricity, transport, as well as for those which are still for the moment hanging on by their fingertips in the public sector, such as health, education and mail delivery. That would be the start.

The second thing would be to organise those involved in the network to reach available communication outlets throughout the media, both paper and electronic, to respond to issues as they arise and put arguments along the lines suggested above. I wouldn't go so far as to rehearse the Obama slogan 'Yes, we can!' – but we could at least try.

Printed in Great Britain
by Amazon.co.uk, Ltd.,
Marston Gate.